Love's Inspiration Saga

Mystic Maiden Warrior's Stories

SHE WALKS WITH WOLVES

By Rick Knowland

Dedicated to Kevin Alexander

The man who loved my sister for over fifty years

See you in heaven bro

1952-2021

Chapter 1

Moon Rising

My name is Moon Rising. I am Cheyenne, The People. I was born sixteen summers ago this very day. I was given my name because I was born as the moon was rising. I am the daughter of Many Coups and Many Robes. My Father received his name because of the many coups he has counted over the years. His Coup Stick that he carries is ten hands long with many scalps of his enemies on it. The Coup Stick that stands in our lodge is over twenty-five hands high, adored with many scalps.

My Father married my mother seventeen summers ago when she was sixteen. He gave my Mother's Father two horses and thirty Buffalo Robes. Thus, her name, Many Robes. I was born in the summer after their marriage. I am their only child. I was born in the Moon of the Buffalo (June) in the Summer of the White Mountain Man (1826).

Today is the Moon of the Buffalo, the Summer Hunt. It is during the Summer of the White Man's Trail (Oregon Trail, 1842). I am riding with my father and five other warriors. Growing up, I did not care to be a traditional Cheyenne woman. Although I can dress a robe, cook, and do all those tasks required of a Cheyenne woman, I was bored with those chores. I listened to my grandfather tell stories of Maiden Warriors. Not common but they did exist. That is what I wanted to become.

That is what my father has trained me to be since I was ten summers old.

This is the beginning of four tasks I must complete before the Moon of Snapping Branches

(December). The first is the Summer Buffalo Hunt. The gathering of meat and skins that will last our Village until the Moon of Harvest (September). That is the second task, the Winter Buffalo Hunt which will provide meat, robes, clothing, and utensils that will last us until next summer. The third task will be my Vision Quest in the Moon of Changing Colors (October). I will not be allowed to partake in the traditional Sun Dance that is done by male warriors of the People. Because that involves skewers run through the chest skin and hung and pulled against the Sun Dance Pole. I will have to go to a sacred place and wait for my Vision. My final task will be in the Moon of Thanks, (November) which will be as a member of a War Party into enemy territory to steal horses.

My Father is the leader of our Village. He stands at least a head taller than any other warrior in our Camp. He is muscular and is very respected within the People. He wears his hair long, past his shoulders with eagle feathers that point in all four of the sacred directions. This shows his status among our Village. He is in love with my mother, and I know she is in love with him. I can hear them every night under their robes. Her sighs and cries. Someday, I will find a man who makes me feel the way my mother feels about my father.

I am considered tall. I stand a little over a head less than my father. I am muscular, long black hair that hangs in a ponytail to my waist, large breasts, and a body full of curves. I wear the loin cloth of a warrior that covers my female bottom area. On my top, I wear a buckskin that presses

my breasts to as flat as possible, held on by sinew straps from a deer, crossing my back and around my neck. My Mother tells me, I am the most beautiful maiden in the Village. Warriors will be lining up to make offers for my hand. But no warrior in this Camp is worthy of this Maiden Warrior.

We make our Village in the sacred Black Hills. My Father is leading us to a meadow where our scouts have found a medium sized herd of Buffalo. We will need to kill about twenty-five adult Buffalo. We will concentrate on bulls and does without calves.

As we near the meadow, My Father has us move downwind from the herd. We dismount and tether our horses. We crawl up the hill and peer out over the meadow. It is a sea of Buffalo. Hundreds of them, grazing in the tall grass. Maheo has blessed us today!

My Father signals for us to move back down the hill to our horses. We mount them and ride downwind coming around the hills and into the meadow, dividing into two groups. With my father in the middle, I ride with two other warriors on the left and three warriors are riding on the right. The Buffalo see us and start a stampede!

Cheyenne Riders are considered the best light calvary riders in the world. I learned to ride from the best! My Father! I have learned to shoot my arrows under my horse's neck or using my legs squeezed around my horse into an upright, standing position in order to shoot an arrow downward into the animal at the base of its neck. Or into the rib cage of the Buffalo. My horse knows my every command, just in the feel of my legs.

I shy away from the straggling Buffalo they are the weak ones. Not much meat. I move to the center of the stampeding herd. I have my lance and bow with a quiver of arrows. I spot a young Buffalo bull and maneuver into him. I take my lance and thrust it into the rib cage. He falls with blood gushing out of his nostrils. I have hit heart and lung! I move on. I see another you bull and move toward him. I push up straight with my bow and arrow ready and fire. Perfect shot at the base of the neck. The bull falls killed instantly.

As the sun rises higher, I killed five more Buffalo before the animal herd disappears over the horizon. In all, we killed thirty-two animals. The women and old arrive from the Village to gut and strip off the animal skins. The warriors will cut the meat so it can be jerked. But large hunks of meat from the rump and shoulder of a couple of the Buffalo are cut for the Buffalo Dance tonight. My Father is very proud of my kills. I have proven to be a worthy hunter. At the Moon of Harvest, I would kill over sixteen Buffalo, one for every summer I have lived.

Chapter 2

The Vision Quest

One day during the Moon of Changing Colors, My Father took me to the edge of the Village. He pointed to a cave up the mountain. I was to go there and start my Vision Quest. He told me the Village would be moving out onto the Plains when the first sliver of the next Moon appears. There should be more than enough time to complete my

Quest. I took no food or water. I wore only my Warrior clothes. No robes for warmth. I reached the cave just as the sun set!

For four days and four nights, I sang my Warrior Songs and prayed to Maheo for my Vision. I was cold, thirsty, and hungry. The walls of the cave grew dark and wavy. I had trouble focusing on my songs or prayers. My vision became even more blurry. I fell into a deep trance.

I stood before a great mist. Out of the mist came a black wolf walking on two legs. The wolf came to me and spoke to me. It was a female voice.

"Rising Moon? Do you understand me?"

"Yes!"

"I am your protector! My name is 'She Who Speaks to the People'! I have come here to give you instructions. First, from this day forward you will be known as 'Mystic Maiden Warrior, She Who Walks with the Wolves'! I will give you powers to be one with wolves. You will be a Protector of the People. You are to go back down after this Vision and tell your Village of all things I will tell you. You will get nourishment and water. On the first day of the next Moon when it is full, you will return to this cave where you will meet a black female wolf who will be your companion for as long as you live. Other wolves will follow you because you will be given special tasks in order to protect the People. The black wolf's name will be 'She Wolf'!

"Before the Moon of Winter White (January), a lone young warrior will ride out of a snowstorm with a lone white wolf following him. His name will be 'Lone Wolf'. He will offer your Father ten of the finest breeding mares for your hand. You will go with him and love him and have four babies. Each one will represent the four sacred directions. You will receive instructions later on this. But Lone Wolf will give you special powers. One that will make you live a very long time. Another to recognize the demons that roam this world among our enemies the Crow, Blackfeet, Shoshoni, and the White Man. Lastly, you husband will give you the ability to drain the life out of those demons. You and your husband will roam this world together to rid Mother Earth of demons. So, the People can live in peace and be fruitful.

"You are to leave with your husband during the Moon of Dripping Leaves (April). You will take no food or water. Only your robes, weapons, and utensils that you will need on your wandering. You will not return to your Village until you have been with child for seven moons. You and Lone Wolf will remain in your Village for many winters. Having your children, raising them, and sending them into the world when they each reach eighteen winters.

"But remember, Maheo has chosen you, Mystic Maiden Warrior, and Lone Wolf to accomplish this mission. The demons are rising and are getting ready to rid this world of the People. You must complete your mission no matter how long it takes. You will live a very long life and will remain sixteen summers, a beautiful, young maiden."

"How can that be?"

"That will be one of the powers given to you by your husband. Now, Mystic Maiden Warrior, it is time to wake up and return to your Village!"

And She Who Speaks to the People turned and walked back into the mist. I awoke, remembering every word.

I went back down the mountain to my Village. I told my Father that I was supposed to talk to all the Camp. He called everyone together and I stood in the center of the circle, surrounded by the entire Village of People. I told them of my Vision. My Father listened.

My Father knew what I was talking about was the truth. Maheo had opened his heart.

"She speaks the truth and I believe her! Maheo has chosen a mighty warrior. I proclaim this day forward that Rising Moon will be known as Mystic Maiden Warrior, She Who Walks with the Wolves!"

My Father was proud of me! I was proud of him for speaking the truth. But from the circle a voice shouted out!

"She lies! She only wants to be a warrior, so she makes up lies about our sacred Vision Quest. She is no warrior. She is a woman and should know her place among the women. Cooking for her husband and giving him babies!"

It was Yellow Horse, a warrior of twenty-one summers. A divorced warrior who wanted me and my body. He was not worthy of me! Then, I saw it! His eyes for an instant were as black as the obsidian stone. Was this my power of recognition?

"Have her show us a sign!"

"I will when I go on the next full moon to get the wolf, She Wolf, and bring her back with me!"

I did not like the smile that crept across Yellow Horse's face. It was evil, like he had a plan against me to end my mission before it started.

When the first full moon rose in the Moon of Thanks, I got up as instructed and left for the cave. The Moon was at its peak, and I arrived at the cave just as the Sun's first light was hitting the sky and clouds. I don't know how I knew but I felt I was being watched and followed. I could not shake the feeling. But someone grabbed me from behind and put a knife to my throat. It was Yellow Horse, and his eyes were as black as obsidian.

"Well, Mystic Maiden Warrior, it appears I have you. I am going to end your mission before it ever starts. But before I slit your throat, I will enjoy your female part several times!

Cheyenne Maidens are taught many things. But one of the things they are taught by their fathers is to protect their virtues at all costs. A Cheyenne Maiden's body is a sacred gift to be given only to the man who marries her. When Yellow Horse eased his grip to cut my loin cloth, I did what I was taught. I stomped on the top of his foot with my heel. He released his grip. I stomped on the other foot, and he dropped his knife. He was jumping up and down in pain!

"I will get you for that!"

A black wolf and I counted eight gray wolves appeared at the mouth of the cave. The wolves looked at Yellow Horse and started snarling with their teeth exposed as they fanned out in order to surround him. Yellow Horse ran and jumped on his horse heading back to the Village. When he got there, he packed everything he could and rode out of the camp.

Once Yellow Horse was gone from the cave, the black wolf came down to me with the gray wolves following. I looked at the black wolf.

"You must be She Wolf?"

The wolf shook its head yes! I could talk to wolves.

"He was a demon, wasn't he?"

She shook her head yes!

"Come, let's get back to the Village!"

We walked into the Village! She Wolf was at my side. One of the gray wolves stopped at the entrance, guarding it. Another lobbed ahead to guard the exit. The six remaining wolves fanned out, three on the left and three on the right. All the gray wolves were guarding the People!

"Father, this is She Wolf! She Wolf, this is my father, Many Coups. And that is my mother, Many Robes!"

She Wolf bowed her head to both my mother and father. She put her head under my hand. I scratched her head!

"She does like me!"

"Mystic, do you know why Yellow Horse left so fast just now?"

"Father, Yellow Horse tried to take my virtue and my life! I did what all Cheyenne Maidens are taught. Protect my virtue! And these guys helped!"

"Taught you well!"

"Yes, you did Father!"

We moved our camp down onto the Plains. She Wolf went with me, and the gray wolves followed at a distance. Five nights later, two of our scouts rode in fast. They had spotted a Crow and Shoshoni Raiding Party with twenty warriors and hundreds of horses. They, also, had the White Man's Firewater!

My Father called a Council of Warriors. We discussed what we needed to do. It was decided that in the morning we would raid the party at first light and steal horses, count coup, and take scalps. We all went to our lodges to sleep and be up before first light.

In a dream, She Who Speaks to the People spoke to me!

"Go now, Mystic Maiden Warrior! Wake all the warriors up. Many Crows are coming to help with the stolen horses and drink the Firewater. They are going to attack the People and carry women and children away. They will kill all the People's Warriors. You are to let the wolves go ahead and scare the Raiding Party and the wolves will stampede the horses. You can count as many coups as you want! But no enemy warrior is to die or be killed by the People. Only Lone Wolf is to determine if the enemy warriors are to die. Do you understand?"

"Yes!"

I woke up my father and told him what She Who Speaks to the People told me. My Father called the warriors together and told them what I had said!

"We have to be concerned with the horses. With many horses we can trade for many things. No killing! Just count coup!"

There was grumbling among the warriors who wanted scalps. I pleaded with them!

"Please heed She Who Speaks to the People's words. I do not know Lone Wolf, but he is to be my husband. She Who Speaks to the

People says he is a great warrior, a Spirit Warrior of Maheo. Please count coup only!"

We rode out when the moon had not peaked. The wolves went ahead of us. We heard yelling among the Crow and Shoshoni Warriors. They ran without their weapons. Horses were heard running and we worked to round them up into some kind of order. We all counted coup on the terrified Crow and Shoshoni. All of us but one!

Lone Knife was chasing a Crow Warrior. He was across the meadow with horses running down the middle! I watched as Lone Knife pulled his knife and threw it into the Crow's back. He pulled it out and rolled the warrior over and plunged the knife into his chest. Then, he took the man's scalp. Lone Knife looked around to see if anyone had seen him. His eyes were obsidian black. I hid myself from his view.

We returned to the Village and counted eighty-two horses. I knew the Crow Party sent to attack us was now out on the Plains trying to find the straggling horses. We now had plenty of horses to ride and trade.

I rode in with six horses that were to be mine. I was now a warrior. My Father announced it to the whole Village. My face was to be painted half white and half black. My body was to have handprints of red on my upper portion. I wore two eagle feathers in my long hair. Gifts from My Father. My horses had black and red handprints on each of their rumps. I was Mystic Maiden Warrior and I counted five coups on my Coup Stick.

Chapter 3

Lone Wolf

Everything that She Who Speaks to the People had come true. Everything but Lone Wolf. I helped my mother with robes and skins. I hunted deer and elk to supplement our food. But I waited for Lone Wolf. The Man I was supposed to marry!

In the Moon of the Snapping Branches, snow started falling. Large flakes, slowly at first and then, the wind blew a driven snow. And that is how it snowed all night. In the morning, the snow was still being blown by the wind.

As I looked out over the snowstorm from our lodge, a lone figure riding a horse with a white wolf at the horse's side came out of the snow. It was a figure with a Buffalo Robe that covered not only his entire body but the body of his horse from the withers to its rump. They were covered in snow, yet they looked warm.

As they entered the Village, the snow stopped! The figure rode towards our lodge. At our lodge, the figure pulled off the Buffalo Robe, shook it out and laid it across the rump of the horse. The man I saw was handsome! The wolf shook itself and the man got down.

My Father came out of our lodge. The man was the same height as my father only the man was more muscular than my father. He presented himself to my Father. He had the most piercing blue eyes I had ever seen. I was in a trance. Then, he spoke! I was His!

"I am Lone Wolf! I have come for your daughter, Mystic Maiden Warrior!"

It was him. His body stirred emotions and fantasies inside me. I kept stealing glances at his loin cloth to get a glimpse of his manhood. I can't explain it, but Lone Wolf made my female area drip. So much my mother noticed a wet spot on my loin cloth and pulled me inside to change.

I desired him! I wanted him! I wanted him to ravage me! All I could think about was feeling him inside me in our marriage robes.

He whistled! Ten magnificent mares came out of the storm that raged all around the Village. It was like the storm surrounded the Village as it continued, yet the Village had no snow.

"Is this sufficient for her hand in marriage?"

"Yes!"

"Then, come let us have a marriage ceremony and feast tonight!"

Two more horses emerged from the storm. Each carrying six large bags. My Father went and checked one of the bags. It contained Buffalo meat! Yes, I was to be married tonight. Oops, dripping female part again!

My Mother dressed me in her White Buckskin Wedding Dress. She pulled my long hair into a ponytail with flowers in my hair and placed wedding moccasins on my feet.

"Daughter, this is your wedding night. Your Warrior will want a magnificent performance. You must remember he cannot be gentle with you. If you are to enjoy this first experience, you must make him thrust into you. Do you understand?"

"Yes, Mother!"

"Let us go and present you to your Husband!"

I hugged my mother! I knew what I had to do, and I desired to mate with my Husband many times.

I was presented to him. We stood before the Village and Sacred Woman, the Shaman, who was to marry us. She said some words that I was not listening to. I was looking into those blue eyes. My female part was starving for him. Sacred Woman gave us a special brew in a cup. It was supposed to be the liquid of life to seal our marriage. It was black and looked and smelled disgusting. But when I put it to my lip, it was sweet and made me feel warm and giddy. It made me want Lone Wolf more. She turned us around and announced us as husband and wife!

The feast began. But I was disappointed! I had not received my first kiss. Ever! I told my mother of my disappointment!

"Mystic, you must understand. Your first kiss with your husband will be in the privacy of your lodge. Because it will lead to more kisses and passion for your husband that will only be satisfied by mating with him. Kissing the first time cannot be in front of the Village. It would lead to your embarrassment."

I now understood! She had seen my desire and my want! She had seen my lust for him. A lust I know was for his love and I had to show him my love for him. I had only met him that afternoon, but I had fallen in love with him when our eyes met. I understood my Vision! I understood what She Who Speaks to the People had told me! "Love him"! And I would for all eternity.

We feasted! I danced for him, over and over again! The Maiden Dance! The Wedding Dance! My Mother took my hand and let me to the Wedding Lodge she and the other women had prepared for us. She kissed my forehead and touched my face and led me to the doorway. Lone Wolf came to me. He lifted the flap for me, and I went in and he followed me in.

I stood before him and removed my moccasins. I started to untie the front of my Wedding Dress, but he came to me and stopped me. He gave me my first kiss. So tender, so soft that when his tongue touched mine, he made me make little cries. I was His!

Chapter 4

The Mate and the Turn

"No, Mystic! We must talk first. We need to know each other before we mate. You know what is coming, don't you? I am to give you powers but you need to know how that is to come about. You need to have knowledge of what that means. You need to trust me for what we will do in the future. I have to teach you and show you who you will be come! I promise we will mate! We will be One with each other! Do you trust me?"

"With my life, Lone Wolf! But you know I desire and want you. It is hard not to mate with you! I need you, Lone Wolf. I am yours! Can't you see that?"

"Mystic, I know! But we must talk! We will do this. We will remove our clothes, hold our naked bodies against each other as we talk. No touching! No mating until we have finished. Are we in agreement?"

"It will be hard! But yes!"

I untied my dress and let it fall to the ground. I stood naked before my husband. The moisture in my female part returned. I saw his desire, his want of me. He removed his loin cloth and stood naked in front of me. I could not take my eyes off his manhood. I wanted it.

I needed it but I held my lust for him within me. I laid naked in our marriage robes in his arms! He asked me

about my life. I told him everything. He smiled and kissed me. I so wanted to mate!

"Mystic! I need to tell you my story so I can prepare you for the powers that I will give you. My story begins a long time ago. Long before you were born, or your parents or grandparents were born. My love, I am a Spirit Warrior!"

I knew what a Spirit Warrior was. My Grandfather had told me the stories. These were Warriors that lived long lives. Hundreds of Summers. They were protectors of the People. They slept during the day and guarded and roamed the earth fighting evil at night. They ate no food or meat. They drank no water. But they drank the blood of our enemies. They were known as Vampires. The human part of me was scared. The woman part was excited.

"I was born in the Moon of New Beginnings (March) in the Summer of the Arrival (1600). I grew up and learned the Warrior's ways. I counted coup, hunted Buffalo, and had my Vision. My Vision did not come to me until my nineteenth Summer in the Summer of the Men with Metal Hats (1619). She Who Speaks to the People came to me in my Vision and told me She would give me powers of the wolves. I would have a companion, a White Wolf called He Wolf. I was to seek out a Spirit Warrior named Fang and give myself to him to receive special powers to become a Spirit Warrior. Then, I was to roam the earth fighting the Evil One and his warriors. At a time in the future, She Who Speaks to the People, would come to me and lead me to the one I was destined to be with. A Maiden Warrior to fight by my side and to bear four children that would fight the demons of this world. Her name would be Mystic Maiden Warrior!"

I could not believe what he told me. Everything She Who Speaks to the People was coming true.

I was falling deeper in love with Lone Wolf.

"Í sought out, Fang, who turned me into a Spirit Warrior. But Fang had brought on disfavor to himself before Maheo. He had taken too many demons in a day that made him crave human blood all the time. He started taking the blood and lives of young maidens. It led to his death as he took the life of a maiden whose brother hunted Fang down and beheaded him.

"I tell you this because after we mate, I will turn you. I will make you a Spirit Warrior, a Vampire. I need to know do you trust me to do that?"

"Yes, My Love! The human part of me is terrified. But the woman part wants you and you alone. And if that is my destiny? I am yours!"

He smiled! He touched my face and kissed me! Again, I was His!

"Alright, Mystic. Here is how our night will be! I will mate with you as a human, twice! So, you can experience our love! Then, I will turn you! That means you will die a human death and awake as a Vampire to feed on my blood in order to turn you into my Vampire Wife. You will have powers beyond your dreams. And I will teach you how to use these powers. Then, you will become one with the wolves. I will show you how that is done. That is so you can walk in the light and the dark. Sleep will be of little use to you! Are you ready, Mystic?"

"Yes, My Love! Please mate with me!"

He started kissing my lips, my neck, and my breasts. I felt his hand run up my thighs and touch my female area. He touched an area with his fingers, and he sucked on one of my nibbles. The sensation was beyond description. It did not take him long to bring out the woman in me. I called

his name and he got between my legs and thrust inside me. There was a moment of pain replaced by a sensation of pleasure. He pushed hard and I felt a growing passion and sensual experience that culminated in a scream. He exploded in me. My very being was part of him. I wanted more. I had never felt the pleasure of the flesh before. It was so amazing! He had to do that to me again!

"Do it again, My Love!"

"Alright! On your stomach, my beautiful wife!"

I did so. He thrust into me from behind. The sensation was twenty times greater than the last. The faster and harder he pushed, the more the intensity of the feeling of pleasure grew inside me. I held onto the edge of our robes. The experience was reaching a peak and it was lasting a long time. I heard him cry out my name and I screamed again! I laid my head on my folded arms. I remembered what he had done to me now twice. He started to withdraw from me.

"Please, My Lover! Stay in me, let me remember as a human woman what you have done to me twice. Then, you will turn me. Please tell me that as a Vampire, we will enjoy mating as we have now?"

"With greater feeling! We will be One just as in human mating!"

That made me smile. He leaned down and whispered in my ear!

"I love you my beautiful wife. It is time!"

He withdrew from me, and I turned over. He was over me, smiling and he kissed me. At that point, I did not care what he did to me as long as I could feel his kisses and love.

He worked his way down to my female part. I could not believe what he did to me next. His tongue went into my female part, and it touched an area that made me arch my back. He worked that area with his tongue. How could such a small part of my body give my entire being so much pleasure? It did not take long for me to call his name. He kissed my female part, and it made me shiver. I felt so limp!

"Trust me, Mystic?"

"With my life, Love!"

He kissed my inner thigh, right where my leg meets my female part. I felt an intense sharp pain that made me cry out. He began sucking. I could feel pleasure, but I felt my life's energy draining from my body. He drank my blood just to the point of death and he stopped.

"I am sorry, my Love! Now you must die as a human and be reborn as a Vampire!"

I felt my life slipping away. It grew darker and darker! Then, here was total blackness. My eyes shot open I took a breath of air! Not really! But I was alive! My stomach turned and I leaned over and threw up the entire contents of it. I assumed my Vampire body was getting rid of anything human in me. I thirsted! Not for water. Blood! I was like an animal. I needed blood, I needed it now! Lone Wolf touched my face! I felt peace come over me!

"Love, come and drink! Bite down on my wrist and drink! I will tell you when to stop!"

Lone Wolf slit his wrist. I bit down, drinking his blood. It was sweet and so delicious. Energy and strength were returning. So, was passion. I drank and drank! I did not want to stop!

"Mystic, enough! Please?"

I let go of his wrist. I felt strong, at peace, and loved. My ears could hear things I never heard before. I could hear long distances and the breathing of the people of my Village as they slept. My eyes could see into the darkness but as though it were light. And I could see far like the objects were right in front of me. And the touch! I had felt

Lone Wolf's touch and love as a human. But as a Vampire, when he touched my face, I felt his love's energy from his body. Every time he touched me, I felt One with him. I could read his mind!

"Amazing, isn't it!"

"Oh, yes! I feel alive and one with Mother Earth!"

He smiled I wanted to look at myself. I grabbed the Looking Glass. There was no reflection. How could that be? I dropped the glass, and it broke. I looked at Lone Wolf, terrified. But he touched me, and all was good again!

"Mystic, we are of the undead! We have bodies but those bodies carry no reflection on glass or streams, or water. You will get used to it!

"Mystic, we need to talk more. You must understand that you will no longer have your bleeding time of the Moon. Most Vampires cannot have children. But Maheo has granted us the ability to have children. Four of them and He has touched you here and planted eggs to be fertilized by me and our love. Those eggs are here and here!"

He touched my body on either side of part that has hair. It aroused passion in me when he did so!

I felt something move from the left side of my part with hair to just above that hair.

"The left side will be boys and the right side will be girls. Northern Warrior and Southern Warrior! Eastern Star and Western Star! They will become great Spirit Warriors. They will find the areas where the demons move from the Evil Place to Earth. They will destroy those places. But tonight, we will conceive Northern Warrior and every two Winters, we conceive the rest!

"We will train them and send them out into the world as we roam the earth finding demons and draining their blood to kill them! We will do that until our children have destroyed the places, I have told you about. Maheo will make us human again and we will love and grow old together!"

That sounded so wonderful!

"But Maheo will want us to use any means to rid as many demons on this earth as possible. You will have the power of seduction. You will use your body to make demons think you want them so we can drain their blood and kill them!"

I got scared!

"Do I have to lie with them?"

"That will be your decision, My Love!"

"I can't Lone Wolf! I can only lie with you; I can only mate with you. I will touch them but that is all. I doubt, I can kiss them! But if I must to protect the People, I will. You need to know I can only make love to you. I love only you, Lone Wolf!"

"Again, that is your decision. And I know you love only me. And it will be hard for me, but Maheo has given us a love that no other man and woman has and we can endure anything! Now, come!

Let as conceive Northern Warrior!"

Lone Wolf lay on his back, and I got on top of him. I inserted him into me. The pleasure was beyond description. The sexual satisfaction was so much greater than as a human. I offered him a nibble and before I knew it, I was screaming him name and he yelled mine! I felt that something above my hair move to my stomach and leap inside my body. I knew Northern Warrior was now inside me.

Lone Wolf got up. He held out his hand to me. I got up and he took me to the robes that were laid out on the other side of our lodge. He had me lay down.

"Mystic! You have turned and become One as a Vampire with me. In order to have the full powers of the Vampires and wolves, you must become one with the wolves!"

"Surely, you do not mean mating with them?"

He laughed!

"Of course not, Mystic! But to communicate with them you must become one with them. Please, trust me?"

I laid there. She Wolf and He Wolf were at my head. They pressed their foreheads against my head. The other eight gray wolves pressed their foreheads against my body!

"Mystic, open your mind. Listen and when you hear their thoughts, use your mind to talk to them!"

I laid there, letting my mind empty. I listened!

"Do you hear me, Mystic Maiden Warrior?" I am She Wolf!"

I could hear her and all the other wolves. It was amazing!

"Yes, I can hear you! Can you hear me?"

"Yes!"

I sat up and the wolves formed a circle around me as She Wolf spoke with her mind!

"I am She Wolf! This is He Wolf!"

"Pleased to meet you!"

"These are Dante, Raul, Rudolph, Markus, Augustus, Brutus, Zeus, and Apollo! We are your and Lone Wolf's protectors. She Who Speaks to the People communicates with us and give us instructions on what demons you Spirit Warriors are to kill! Do you understand?"

"Yes!"

"Good! Because prepare yourself for a demon is coming for you Mystic!"

I looked surprised! I got up and went and laid with Lone Wolf, remembering what She Wolf had told me. I was happy and I felt powerful! She Wolf laid next to me with her head up and she was alert. I touched my stomach I felt a stirring inside me. Northern Warrior! I received a very tender kiss from my husband. I could hear Mother Earth's creatures moving about! I was at peace! I was loved!

She Wolf snapped to her feet, looking at the opening of our lodge. My eyes shot open. I was not sleeping but merely taking in my husband's love. I could sense it. A power was moving outside of our lodge. How did I know this? I could see who it was. Lone

Knife, a demon!

Chapter 5

The Frank Drummond Brothers

Lone Wolf was alert. He pressed his finger to his lips to be quiet.

He gave me a knife. One whose blade was made of silver. He

motioned for me to lay on the robes. Exposed and naked! He stood

by the entrance. A lone figure walked into our lodge. It was Lone

Knife!

"Ah, I see your husband is not with you Mystic Maiden Warrior!

Maybe I will take you before I kill you before your mission ever

starts."

His smile was evil! I knew he intended to do me harm. I sat up!

The knife's blade gleaming in the moonlight. He saw the silver.

"Do you think you can overpower me? I am strong and you are a

mere woman. No match for my strength. No, I think I will take your multiple times before I slit your throat. I am a demon. You are mortal. Who can save you mortal woman?"

"I can, Lone Knife! Prepare to die!"

It was Lone Wolf, and he sank his fangs into Lone Knife's neck and drank his blood. Lone Knife grew weak. My husband raised his head!

"Come, my wife, feast on this demon. Finish him off!"

I came to the demon who was trying to protest. I sank my vampire fangs into the place where Lone Wolf had started drinking. I drank and drank. The power of the demon flowed into my body. I felt invincible. Northern Warrior stirred in my womb. He was rejoicing in the death of a demon. I drank every last drop of that demon's blood. I threw his dead body down. He turned to dust. My mouth and chin were covered in blood. But I needed my husband. I needed to mate! She Wolf looked at me!

"Go, lie with your husband! Then, we talk!"

You know the thing about Vampires and wolves is that we are not mortal enemies. We tolerate each other. Vampires are reactive, we use brute force, and think we know all the answers. Wolves, on the other hand, are cunning, strategists. They think through the situation as it happens and form a plan for it before it needs a plan. Vampires don't see the plan until long after a plan is needed.

The reason She Who Speaks to the People brought Lone Wolf and I together with the wolves, was the need for a combined force. She recognized that we and our children would get the mission accomplished. It would be the wolves who formed the plans. We worked as a team. No matter how far apart we were from the wolves, they always talked to us with their minds. They planned, we executed! It was an amazing relationship and love for one another! They were our best friends!

I laid there with my husband after amazing sex that had shown our love. I felt so strong. Lone Wolf was stroking my bottom. I felt his love in his touch. She Wolf was still waiting for us. I thought!

"Sorry, lost in the moment! What do you want to talk to us about She Wolf?"

"Mystic, we must talk. I have the next demons that need to die at your hands!"

I sat up. I pulled my knees against my naked body. I listened!

"There are six brother demons known as the Frank Drummond Brothers. They are White Men who are very evil demons. They are stealing and forcing themselves on young maidens of the Whites and of the People. They are trying to get maidens with child. To raise demon children with special powers to kill the Spirit Warriors.

"They have stolen three Crow maidens. Sapphire, Jasmine, and Rose. The Drummond Brothers keep them in the nearby town in a building where they force themselves on those maidens daily. Maheo has made them barren. And the brothers will grow tired of them and kill them. Your mission is to kill the brothers and return the maidens to their Village!"

"But they are Crow! Our enemies! They will try to kill us!"

"No, they will not! They will rejoice in the maidens return. Besides, there are only two ways to kill Spirit Warriors. Cut off their head or have a wooden stake driven into their heart. You will be safe!

"The Drummond Brothers ride in pairs. Frank with Jacob, Tyler with Scott, and Michael with David. Two brothers always remain with the maidens while the other two pair go in opposite directions to steal and rape!

"You two will follow Frank and Jacob. They are the head of the demon snake! You will lure them into the woods. Mystic, you will seduce them to think you will mate with them. Take Frank into the woods. Let him touch you and you touch him, but you will not sleep with him. When you have him in a state that he thinks he will mate with you, you will attack! You will suck all his blood from his body and toss his dead body aside.

"Lone Wolf, you will stay with Jacob. He will hear Frank's cries as Mystic takes his blood. Jacob will think Frank is enjoying Mystic and will want to watch. As he walks by you, Lone Wolf, you will take his blood.

"Their bodies will turn to dust, so take their clothes and hide them. David and Michael will follow the next day in the direction that Frank and Jacob went. Mystic, you will lure them and seduce them as you did Frank and Jacob. You and Lone Wolf will take their blood. Scott and Tyler will try to find their brothers. They will bring the Crow maidens with them with the intention of killing them. That is when you and Lone Wolf will strike. You will kill them, taking their blood. Lone Wolf and Mystic, you will return the maidens to their Village. Do you understand?"

I thought! Touching them and letting them touch me? Disgusting!

"Mystic Maiden Warrior, do you understand?"

I looked indignant!

"Yes! But I am not going to like it!"

"Maheo knows that. That is why He makes it so disgusting for you!"

"Great!"

It was the Moon of Dripping Leaves (April) when we left my Village. I said goodbye to my father and mother. We rode out of the Village taking only our weapons, robes, and utensils we might need along our journey. We took no food or water which my parents thought quite odd.

Today we rode not as husband and wife. We rode as Spirit Warriors. Our faces were painted half white and half black. This signifies day and night. Around our eyes were circles of red. Spirit Warriors! I wore moccasins with deerskin leggings split up the back of my legs and a loin cloth. I had on a deerskin shirt that was big on me. My hair was in a ponytail that hung to my bottom. It had seven eagle feathers that traveled from the top of my ponytail to its tip. They were my wedding gift from Lone Wolf. One eagle feather pointed upward out of the knot of my ponytail. This pointed to the heavens. The bottom eagle feather pointed to the ground. Mother Earth!

Lone Wolf wore the same as I did. Except he wore only two eagle feathers. One pointed to the heavens and one pointing to the earth. He rode a black stallion and led two black bay horses. He had one loaded with robes. The White Wolf, He Wolf, walked beside him and his horse.

I rode a palomino with red handprints on it, a Spirit Horse. I, too, led two horses. One white, a gray, and one a paint. Each had robes and other supplies on them. The Black Wolf, She Wolf, walked beside me and my horse.

Lone Wolf carried his Spirit Shield strapped to his back. Strapped to it were his lance with the silver blade. A tomahawk with a silver head and his bow. On the horse, he carried his Coup Stick and a quiver of arrows with silver heads. On his left hip was the knife with the silver blade. On

his right hip was an ordinary knife for everyday use. Sharp enough to scalp our enemies.

I, too, carried a Spirit Shield strapped to my back. I had a tomahawk with a silver head strapped to the shield along with my bow. My

Coup Stick and a quiver of arrows with silver tips were hung on my horse. I carried on my left hip a knife with a silver blade and on my right hip an ordinary knife. My Father offered us a long gun of the Whites'! But Lone Woof thought it too heavy!

He Wolf and She Wolf walked at our sides. Raul and Augustus walked several hundred yards ahead of us, scouting. Brutus and Zeus stayed several hundred yards behind us. The rest, three on the left and three on the right, were several hundred yards away from us. Guarding us! Protecting us!

Our destination was Deadwood Falls which was less than a morning's ride to the town. Lone Wolf had been told, the Drummonds had moved into town and killed the sheriff. They now ruled the town.

The wolves' plan was simple. We would wait for Frank and Jacob to find us at the Falls. When we saw them coming from a longways off, I would bathe naked in the Falls and come out as they approached. I would seduce them into thinking I would mate with each of them. But I would kill Frank and Lone Wolf would kill Jacob.

It took us until the sun almost reached its peak to reach the Falls. We set up our camp. We waited and watched!

We were there three days when I saw them coming. They were several miles from us! I stripped naked and got into the pool of the Falls. Lone Wolf hid in the woods that surrounded the Falls.

As they approached, I walked out of the pool. I saw their obsidian eyes. I saw them drool. It made my skin crawl!

"Well, well, well, squaw! Where is your Man?"

I stood there naked, wringing out my long hair!

"Out hunting! Won't be back for a while!"

"Well, sounds like a good time to get acquainted with your pussy!"

That must be what the White Man called a woman's female part. I kind of liked that name. I would have to tell Lone Wolf. I wanted him right now!

"Come on squaw! Lay on your back and let me mate with you!"

"Slow down cowboy!"

I used the name Lone Wolf told me to use to slow their lust for me!

"I will mate with both of you. But one at a time. I would rather go into the woods and mate against a tree. Makes it better for me! Makes me want to be ravaged more!"

How disgusting! I wiggled my finger at Frank and walked towards the woods. Once inside, I leaned against a tree!

"Touch me here!"

I touched my breasts!

"So, I can get ready for you! Take off your pants so I can get you hard enough for me. I require a very hard manhood!"

My stomach turned!

Frank touched my breasts! I saw his obsidian eyes get even darker. I unbuttoned his long underwear. I put both my hands into them and wrapped my hands around his manhood and manhood sack! Yuck!

"How does that feel, Cowboy?"

"Wonderful! When do I get to poke you?"

"I am almost ready! Just a little while longer!"

Jacob would no longer wait. He wanted to watch and then, poke me!

"Frank hurry up! I want my poke! Just don't make her pussy too sloppy for me!"

I removed my hands. There was some of his manhood juices on them! I almost threw up! He thought it was time to poke me. I smiled and showed him my fangs and plunged them into Frank's neck and started drinking. Jacob walked up to us and when he saw me drinking Frank's blood, Jacob screamed!

"Vampire!"

He looked for something to kill me with. But he had not seen what I had seen. My husband behind

him. He grabbed Jacob and plunged his fangs into his neck and drank. We drank all their blood. I felt so strong when finished. We both were covered from our mouths to our chins with blood. We tossed their dead bodies aside. I needed Lone Wolf! I needed him to cleanse me of what I had to touch and endure. I needed cleansing! Frank and Jacob's bodies turned to dust. The one thing I remembered as I drank Frank's blood were his eyes. They were black! Then, they turned gray. Finally, they turned white. All of Frank's life had been drained from his body.

I ran to the pool and jumped in. I had to wash the disgusting stink of Frank off of me. His juices, his filth!

Lone Wolf stripped and walked into the pool. He came up to me. I was obsessed with cleaning myself. He touched my face! I looked into his loving eyes and became very calm. He cleaned my face and my hands. He kissed me and kissed me. Before I knew it, we were calling each other's names. He had cleansed me inside and out! I so loved my Warrior!

We lay under our robes. I felt loved! I snuggled against Lone Wolf. We were One again. No man would ever be One with me. Never! We talked!

"Mystic! We need to go down to the town. We have to find the maidens and talk to them. You have to talk to them. Tell them the wolves' plan so we kill all the Drummond Brothers!"

We got dressed. Lone Wolf wore nothing but a loin cloth and moccasins. I did the same but with a tight cloth, pressing my breasts against me. We rode to town.

Once in town, we went to the building where we thought the Drummonds held the maidens. We

were right! We sensed they were there. We saw the four other brothers. They were talking!

"Where are Frank and Jacob, David?"

"If I know them, they are enjoying a young girl's pussy. Probably shacked up with her or them making sure they are pregnant! Michael, you and I will head west and try to find them. Maybe we can get some of that pussy!"

"Alright! First light!"

Lone Wolf and I made our way to the back stairs that led up to the next level. No one was guarding it. Lone Wolf went down the hall to just before the stairs. As he walked down the hall, he sensed the maidens and pointed at their door. He stood guard! I knocked on the door. A young maiden opened it. Two other maidens sat on the bed, holding tightly to each other!

"Yes?"

"Which are you? Sapphire, Jasmine, or Rose?"

"Sapphire! How do you know our names?"

"We are here to rescue you!"

"You are Cheyenne! We are Crow! We are your enemies! Why help us?"

"Because no man should ever force himself on a maiden!"

Sapphire started to cry. I held her. Who knew what unspeakable things those brothers had done to them! Standing there She Wolf spoke to me laying out a new plan. A plan I liked so much better! I motioned for Lone Wolf to come into their room. When he got there, I gave him a tender

kiss.

"My Love, She Wolf has a plan!"

I laid out her plan! How to kill all four of the brothers without leaving this building! Lone Wolf stood there and then, he smiled.

"Good plan! At least you won't have to seduce any of them!"

"Okay, Sapphire. Can you and Jasmine seduce David and Michael into other rooms?"

"Yes!"

"Then, take David next door. I will hide while you get him into bed. Jasmine, you will do the same across the hall. Lone Wolf will hide there. No matter what happens, you cannot scream when we kill them. Do you understand?"

"Yes!"

"Good! Let's get rid of these scumbags!"

I kissed Lone Wolf and pressed my forehead against his! I was so in love with him!

"I love you, my husband!"

"I love you, Mystic!"

We kissed again! I turned to Sapphire and Jasmine!

"You know what you need to do! Do it!"

Sapphire went out first and opened the door next to the room the girls were in. She went to the top of the stairs. She leaned on the railing looking down on the saloon they were in. It had a few tables and chairs but mostly the few men who were in there, were at the bar. Sapphire saw David and looked at him seductively!

"David! I am lonely! I need a poke!"

Jasmine came up beside Sapphire!

"Me, too! Michael, I can't start poking without you!"

David and Michael looked at each other! They smiled and chuckled!

"There's going to be a lot of pokin' tonight!"

Tyler and Scott looked at the girls!

"What about us? Where's Rose?"

"You know it is her bleeding time of the Moon! When we are done with these two, we will be back for you!"

"David, don't make it sloppy for me!"

"I make no promises, Tyler!"

David and Michael bounded up the stairs as Sapphire and Jasmine disappeared into the rooms with open doors. David came to the doorway and Sapphire was naked on the bed. He started chuckling and closed the door. His black, obsidian eyes met mine!

"What the fuck?"

I grabbed David by the shoulders and sank my fangs into him. Sapphire watched in horror as I drained David of his blood. His eyes went from black to white. David was dead. I dropped his lifeless body to the floor. My whole lower portion of my face was covered in blood. Sapphire looked like she was going to scream. I put my finger to my lips to let her know to be quiet. Her eyes were wide. I washed my face off in the water basin. David was now a lump of dust under his clothes. I looked at Sapphire.

"You, okay?" We have two more to kill!"

"Yes but scared!"

"I know! Now go and get Tyler!"

Sapphire wrapped a sheet around herself and went to the staircase.

"Tyler, you ready? We'll need to use another room I wore David out!"

Tyler giggled and started up the staircase. Sapphire went into another room and laid naked on the bed. Tyler came in starting to undress. He heard Jasmine tell Scott the same as Sapphire had told him. Tyler shut the door and did not notice me! Not until I sank my fangs into his neck. He tried to cry out but could not. I drained him of his blood. He was a lump of dust.

Lone Wolf came out of another bedroom. He had taken care of Michael and Scott. The maidens got dressed and we snuck out the back stairway. On the street, no one noticed us. I looked at Sapphire!

"Where are their horses?"

"Over there!"

She pointed to four horses hitched to a post. Lone Wolf untied their bridles and led them away. No one protested!

Soon we were out of town, headed for our camp. The girls rode the Drummond horses. At the camp, we now had six extra horses. These would be gifts to the girls' fathers. We stripped the saddles off the horses and hid them.

In the morning, we mounted our horses, the girls led a horse each as we rode out. They guided us to where they thought their Village might be. When we neared the campsite, we were surrounded by Crow Warriors. At first, they were going to try to kill us until they saw the girls. They took us to the leader of the Village, Scar!

Scar was the Father of Jasmine and Rose. He was happy to see them. They told him of their ordeal. The Crow Warriors started to crowd around us. That was until the wolves surrounded the Warriors. Snarling and snapping their teeth! The Crow moved back and realized we were powerful. Scar saw our shields! He was afraid! Spirit Warriors!

We talked to Scar and Buffalo Man, Father of Sapphire. I told them of their daughters' bravery. Scar and Buffalo Man decided to have a feast and dance. Lone Wolf and I sat back in the shadows and watched the Crow. We noticed five or six demons among the Crow. It appeared they were plotting our destruction.

After the Village went to sleep, Lone Wolf and I gathered our robes and packed our horses. We rode out of the Village unnoticed by anyone. By mid-day sun, we were far away from the Crow Village. We wandered and waited for our next adventure!

Chapter 6

The Children

My belly grew and grew! I was happy! I was in love! I so enjoyed my husband's love. We roamed for many moons. In the Moon of the Wallowing Buffalo (July), I was seven moons with child. I wore my small buckskin top and deerskin leggings.

Lone Wolf felt we needed to find my Father's Village. So, I could give birth! My only concern was we would be there a long time. I was to birth four babies in eight summers. Then, there would be the training. Lone Wolf told me it was necessary, and we would survive. I knew I could survive anything as long as he was at my side!

We rode into the Village. Everyone looked at us not believing that we rode with wolves. My Mother ran to my horse. I climbed down and hugged her. She was not appreciative of my dress. She produced an oversized deerskin dress which I protested about. Actually, it was quite comfortable.

We camped just outside the Village. That was because of the wolves. We noticed no demons among our Village. I bided my time, waiting for Northern Warrior's birth. He came in the Moon of Harvest (September). He was perfect!

When I started nursing him, I noticed what I produced from my breasts was not milk. It was blood! I had to hide him under a cloth so my mother would not see it! I used the excuse that I was shy about exposing myself to anyone but my husband. Northern Warrior nursed for fifteen moons. That was when I felt a movement from the right side of the hair over my female part to just above that hair. I remembered what Frank Drummond had called it! My pussy! Always made me giggle when I heard that word. By Northern Warrior's eighteenth moon, I was with child. Eastern Star!

During the time before Northern Warrior's birth, in one of those rare moments, I fell asleep. She Who Speaks to the People came to me. She told me that Lone Wolf and I must stay with my People. I was to give birth to all four of the children that Lone Wolf had told me about. We were to train them to be Warriors. They were going to destroy the places where the demons moved free between the Evil Place and Earth. There would come a time when She Who Speaks to the People would come to me with a new mission. It would be many Winters before that happened. In a way I was relieved that I did not have to be seductive to lure demons to their death. I still remembered what I had to do to Frank Drummond. It made me cringe!

The White Man began roaming into our territory. We ran many off, but they kept coming. A steady stream of people, like the snake slithering across the land. I could not believe their numbers. It was during this time that we learned of the White Man's obsession of time. For the People there was no time. There was no possession of land. The sun came up in the East and it went down in the West. Months were Moons. Years were Winters or Summers. We measured the height of the sun with a reference to its position in the sky which was the part of day it was. But White Men used watches and clocks to measure their day. Moons were months. Winters or Summers were years. So, we adapted to their measurement.

We now kept our time or Moons as the White Man's months. The Moon of Winter White was January. The Moon of Melting Snow, February. March was the Moon of New Beginning. April, the Moon of Dripping Leaves. The Moon of New Blossoms was May. The Moon of the Buffalo, June. July was the Moon of Wallowing Buffalo. August, the Moon of the Sun's Heat. The Moon of Harvest was September. The Moon of Changing Colors, October.

November was the Moon of Thanks. And finally, December, the Moon of Snapping Branches.

Northern Warrior was born in 1843. Eastern Star would be born in 1845. Southern Warrior would arrive in 1847. And Western Star would birth in 1849. Everyone was born between September 9 and 19! I so enjoyed giving birth to each of them. I enjoyed making them even more.

She Who Speaks to the People had told me in my dream that our children would be the first Vampire Children born of the People. They would probably be the last. Until their sixteenth Winter, they would only live on animal blood. On the date of their sixteenth year of their birth, they would drink of either my blood or Lone Wolf's blood. They would seek their Vision Quest afterward.

The male children were to seek their Visions the traditional way. Hanging from the Sun Dance Pole by leather tethers hooked to bone skewers in their chests. The skin would either break or they had their Vision still hanging. Northern and Southern Warriors hung, and their skin never broke. The females were to seek their Vision like I had, the Sacred Cave.

She Who Speaks to the People would come to each of them and speak to them of their mission.

Wolves would be their protectors and their planners. Lone Wolf was to provide eagle feathers for each of our children. Northern Warrior being the eldest, would be the Protector of his brother and sisters. He was to wear four eagle feathers like my Father's. Each pointing in the sacred directions. The other children were to wear one eagle feather facing the direction for which they were named.

Once our children turned sixteen winters, their sleeping habits would become like ours. They would rarely sleep. Lone Wolf and I enjoyed each other's bodies early every morning and late at night. When the children started to turn sixteen, making love to my husband became more challenging. Not being able to enjoy my husband's body each morning and night made Mystic a very unhappy female. We had to steal away at night and make love on the ground, against trees or rocks, or in streams. Not as comfy as in our soft robes. Don't get me wrong, any place, any time with my husband was wonderful. But soft, comfy, sweet love from him was to live for. But the wolves gave us an idea. When Northern Warrior turned sixteen, I put up a lodge for him and eventually his brother.

When Eastern Star turned sixteen, I put up a lodge for her and eventually her sister. In the end, it gave Lone Wolf and I the privacy we needed. Mystic became a very happy female. And my female part was so happy!

Chapter 7

Sand Creek

We heard that in April, 1861, the White Men went to war against each other. Most of the People prayed the Whites would kill each other off. I knew that would not be possible. But many would die. At least we did not see many Whites traveling the trails west.

In 1859, Northern Warrior had his Vision Quest. He hung for hours without breaking his skin. She Who Speaks to the People came to him and told Northern Warrior that the wolves, Zeus and Augustus, were to become his protectors. That his Father would make him a Spirit Shield, a lance with a silver blade, a tomahawk with a silver blade, and a special knife with a silver blade, as well. She told him that when he turned eighteen summers, he was to leave his mother and father and travel north and wander the northern lands of the earth.

After many moons, he would ride into a Cheyenne Village and there he would find his Mate, Morning Star. He was to turn her and together they would seek out the Northern Portal that the demons used to go between the Evil Place and Earth. They would have no children and would probably take many years, possibly centuries to locate that Portal and destroy it.

Northern Warrior told us of his Vision and Lone Wolf prepared the weapons that Northern Warrior had been told to secure from his Father. Lone Wolf, also, gave Northern Warrior four eagle feathers for his hair.

In late November 1864, I fell asleep! As always, She Who Speaks to the People came to me frantic.

"Mystic awake! Hurry get Lone Wolf, gather your children. Gather your weapons and take two horses each with you. Ride without haste to a place where the Sand Creek bends at a huge sand bar in what is called Southeastern Colorado. There is a Village of Cheyenne and Arapahoe, mostly women and children camped there. The demons are going to descend on them with the intent to wipe them out. They are camped with Black Kettle. Please, you cannot stop it! Save as many as you can. They plan to attack the day before the end of the Moon of Thanks. Make haste!"

She faded! I awoke Lone Wolf, Southern Warrior, and Western Star, telling them of my Vision. I sent She Wolf after Northern Warrior and Eastern Star. Lone Wolf gathered two horses each. We painted our faces for war! Half white, half black! Seven eagle feathers in my ponytail. Eagle feathers in Southern Warrior's and Western Star's hair. And two eagle feathers in Lone Wolf's hair. We wore buckskin shirts and leggings with moccasins. We wore long Buffalo Robes that kept our horses warm. We took only our shields, tomahawks, and knives because we had to travel light. With all our wolves, we rode at a fast trot.

We stopped frequently to rest the horses and switched between the horses we were leading. She Who Speaks to the People had told me the camp would be attacked in seven days. We rode for days. We arrived on the day the attack was to take place. We arrived before daybreak. The Camp was surrounded by Blue Coats. We could not stop the attack!

We searched for an escape route, and it was the wolves who found one, undercover to the south of

the Camp. The People would have to wade into Sand Creek which was probably cold. But if we could save many of their lives, it would be worth it.

We looked at the Blue Coats from undercover. Many had obsidian eyes. The darkest belonged to their leader. We heard later that his name was John Chivington. What a brave man to attack women and children. I wanted to send him to the depths of the Evil Place where he belonged. We later learned there were almost seven hundred soldiers there. At dawn, the attack started!

Women and children were screaming. They were cut down by the rapid firing. They were unarmed. Black Kettle came out of his lodge that had the American Flag in front, trying to get the soldiers to stop. His efforts made little difference. The soldiers kept firing.

Lone Wolf and Southern Warrior got the attention of the fleeing People and guided them into the water and I and Western Star showed them on to the shore and a place that would keep them safe. The wolves formed a corridor to that place. They were protecting them.

I saw Black Kettle among those fleeing. How sad! He had called for peace at all costs with the Whites. This was how they repaid his efforts! It made me so angry. I had to turn my deep red eyes from those on shore.

We saved many but many died. We heard the estimates of those killed were between seventy and seven hundred. I believe it was the higher number. Most were women and children. Their Leader sat on his horse his eyes so black. He was smiling. I so hated him!

But what disgusted me the most was what those demons did to the dead. The People would have never done what they did to women and children. I could never describe it. It made me so sick.

We were told later these demons even displayed their trophies at a major gathering place in Denver.

How awful!

They dug pits and threw the People's bodies into them. I cried for them! Such a waste of lives. Lives cut short. No human being deserved to be treated like those bodies were treated. Bodies disfigured, babies cut from their mothers' wombs, missing body parts. It sickens me whenever I remember. I wanted to kill all seven hundred of those bastards! And we did kill some of those demons. At least we did avenge a few of the dead People!

It took far longer for the soldiers to clean up what they had done to the People than the actual massacre lasted. Once the pits were covered, the soldiers searched for their dead. They found none. So, they rode out of the smoldering Village. They were laughing and talking. They drank Fire Water like they were celebrating the success of a hunt. I could no longer hold my emotions within me. I sat down and cried for a long time. I only stopped crying after Lone Wolf took me into his arms. I felt safe and loved. But I saw his tears. We were both angry but there was nothing that could be done about it.

As the soldiers rode away, we noticed a small group of soldiers break away, heading east! I assumed they were heading towards the new fort that was being built to protect the Whites that would begin traveling the trails headed west. Fort Hays! We would remember that group of demons. We would kill them one day to avenge what they had done to the People!

But for now, we took the survivors and headed west, back to our Village. There, my father and the Villagers shared what they had with them. When they were strong enough, Black Kettle took his People and headed south and east. Our paths would cross again in four years. Not a good

crossing!

As the soldiers rode back to their city called Denver, we watched their Leader, John Chivington. It was told to us later that he was a Man of the Cloth, a pastor. How could a man who tells people of his God, do such horrible things to other human beings? Of course, the White Man did not consider The People as human beings. We were savages! But I know this was not their God. This was demons. Just like most Whites' in authority, this was about power. We learned that John Chivington aspired to be governor of Colorado and may be Senator to the place where the Great Father lived, Washington!

But what he had done was an act of cowardice! That is what the powers that be in Washington wrote about him and it killed any political aspirations. He claimed the Cheyenne fired first. But it was the Blue Coats that fired first and what few guns the People had were no match for the fire power of the soldiers.

Chivington left Colorado not long after Sand Creek and moved to the Midwest to continue his false preaching. He would return to

Colorado later in life and spread false talks. Thirty years after Sand Creek, Northern Warrior would avenge those massacred. He would take Chivington's blood!

Chapter 8

The Children Continued

Northern Warrior

Northern Warrior turned eighteen in September 1861. On the day of his birth, September 16, he painted his face black with white around his eyes. This signified his direction, the North. He was the Northern Spirit Warrior! In fact, each of our children would have their own war paint as given to them by She Who Speaks to the People.

Eastern Star would paint her face white with red around her eyes. This would be the Rising Sun from the east. She would be the Eastern Spirit Warrior. Southern Warrior would paint his face yellow with green around his eyes. He would be the New

Beginning, the Southern Spirit Warrior. Finally, Western Star would paint her face red with black around her eyes. She was the Setting Sun, the Western Spirit Warrior. This was how each of our children left our Village. This is how each faced their demons in the years they roamed this earth.

But today, Northern Warrior left our lodge. I was sad to see him go but happy for him. He rode out riding a black and white Paint horse. He led a white and brown Paint and a red and white Paint horses. He carried the shield and weapons on his body. His coup stick and quiver of arrows were on his Paint. I hugged him and let him ride out of sight. Zeus and Augustus walked with him. One on either side of him. I had learned the reason why eight wolves followed us. Two of each would leave with each of our children as their protectors. As the last of the gray wolves left us, two wolves would arrive to replace them. One black and one white. They were to help She Wolf and He Wolf protect us.

Before Northern Warrior left, Lone Wolf put his hand on Northern Warrior's shoulder. Lone Wolf looked into his son's eyes and nodded to him. Acknowledging his son as a Warrior. A Father showing his love for his son!

Northern Warrior rode for many moons. He killed deer, antelope, Mountain Sheep, and Buffalo along his journey. He always left his kills after drinking their blood at a nearby Village. It did not matter what Nation the Village was! Friend or foe! He left it for the old and women and children. No one stopped him or tried to kill him.

Northern Warrior would kill an enemy once a week to satisfy his thirst for human blood. On this particular day in December 1863, it started to snow. By late afternoon it was blowing, accumulating snow. He was in an area of what is known as Wyoming. He had killed a deer, drank its blood. He sensed a nearby Village. A Village of the People. Northern Warrior wore no war paint, he was the man that he was as he rode into that Village in the blinding snow. Morning Star sensed someone was coming! She walked out of the lodge she shared with her parents and siblings. She stood in the middle of the Village in her Buffalo Robe. It was cold and

her robe was accumulating snow. But it stopped snowing in the Village. Around the Village it still snowed but not one flake fell in that Camp. Out of the snow came a lone figure on a Painted horse with two wolves walking beside him. It was him, Northern Warrior, the one she was waiting for. It was the man she was to marry. She removed her robe so he could see her and fall in love with her as she was! She needed him to remove his robe for her desire for him was great. She wanted to see the man that would make her his woman! Northern Warrior saw her. He knew in an instant that this was Morning Star. The woman who would be his wife. She was dressed in a buckskin dress that hugged her body. She was almost as beautiful as I was. A maiden of sixteen Winters with flawless skin, long, jet black hair that hung past her shoulders. She was not as breasted as I was, but her breasts were desirable. She had curves like me. His desire for her was great. He rode to her and looked into her eyes. He saw her want of him. This was the love of his life!

"You must be Morning Star?"

"Yes! You must be Northern Warrior?"

"Yes! Where is your father?"

"This way!"

She smiled at him. She wanted to touch his face. She wanted to kiss him. She needed to mate with him on their wedding robes. She knew he was a Spirit Warrior. She wanted to be like him for all eternity. She led him to her parent's lodge. To her father, Bear

Hunter, the warrior who had killed a bear with only a knife. Bear Hunter came out of his lodge. He was much shorter than

Northern Warrior who was tall and muscular. Bear Hunter knew who Northern Warrior was.

"Spirit Warrior, what do you want?"

"To ask for your daughter's hand in marriage!"

"I know what you are! Why would I give my daughter into your hands?"

"To be my wife and Maiden Warrior! To be my companion on my quest to fulfill Maheo's wish to destroy demons!"

Bear Hunter looked at his daughter. He saw the lust for Northern Warrior, but he also saw her love for him. It was a lust of the body but the want of Northern Warrior's love. He understood that desire. It was the same desire that her mother had for him. To please him. To be with him! He sighed!

"What are your prepared to offer me for her?"

Northern Warrior whistled and ten fine young mares of different colors appeared out of the snowstorm and stood before Bear Hunter. Fine breeding stock!

"These!"

"Then, it is done! Today, Morning Star marries you, Northern Warrior! Tonight, we feast, and you and Morning Star become husband and wife!"

Morning Star could not contain herself. She smiled and leapt into Northern Warrior's arms and kissed him!

"Tonight, I will become yours forever!"

The marriage of Northern Warrior and Morning Star was completed! The feast and Wedding Dance was done. They were led to the lodge that had been erected by the women of the Village for them. They were left alone outside their lodge. Northern Warrior gave Morning Star a very soft and tender kiss. Morning Star was His!

They went into their Wedding Lodge. Morning Star took off her Wedding Dress and moccasins. She stood naked in front of Northern Warrior. He removed his shirt and pants. She looked at his hard manhood and wanted him. He desired her. Morning Star looked at Northern Warrior.

"My Love, you cannot be gentle! Please let me enjoy our first experience!"

"I know my darling! I just do not want to hurt you!"

"It will be for just a moment. And then, the pleasure will begin! But I know who you are and what you are. The pain of our first mating will be nothing compared to the pain when you turn me. But in the end, it will be worth being with you for all eternity!"

"It pains me to have to turn you, Morning Star. I am so in love with you. I know this is how it will be! Please forgive me for what I must do to you!"

There were tears in his eyes. At that moment Morning Star knew he loved her. She touched his face and kissed him, over, and over again!

"Come my husband! Make me your woman. Let me enjoy you as a human woman as many times as you want me! Then, make me your Vampire bride for all eternity. Make me the woman I will become for you every day of our lives together!"

She took his hand and led him to their Wedding Robes. She pulled him down on top of her between her legs. She grabbed his manhood and thrust it inside her, hard. At first there was a pain and then, the pleasure! He pushed very hard inside her. She had trouble breathing, it felt so good. She felt a building of her pleasure. She smiled she knew it was coming. She felt him grow harder, the knowledge of that made her mind explode. She cried out and the feeling kept coming, it did not subside. She buried her head into his shoulder. Northern Warrior cried out her name. He was still slowly pushing inside her. Each push released another gasp, another feeling of pleasure. He was magnificent! That was the most amazing experience she had ever felt. She wanted more!

Northern Warrior made love to her twice more. Each time was better than the others. Morning Star could not get enough of him. Finally, Morning Star had Northern Warrior lay on his back and she climbed on top of him. She did not insert him into her. She offered him a nibble!

"Northern Warrior, drink! Then, turn me, my love!"

Norther Warrior took her breast in his mouth. Morning Star inserted him into her so she could feel him as a human woman one last time. She felt a sharp pain in her breast as he drank her blood. Darkness and the lack of energy fell over her. He drank until just before the point of death. Everything was black! Her eyes shot open! He was still inside her. She thirsted for blood, but she thirsted for his manhood. Northern Warrior took his knife and cut open a place on his chest!

"Drink Morning Star until I tell you to stop!"

He got into a rhythm with her. She drank his blood. The more she drank, the faster their motion

became. At a point that Northern Warrior was going to pull her head away, Morning Star let go of his chest. She cried his name as he cried hers. They were now One as Vampires!

The lower portion of her face was covered in blood. They kissed with a passion neither had known before. Their love for each other had grown. She soon discovered her powers, as a Vampire! She knew they would have to leave soon because her parents and the People would not understand that she was now a Spirit Warrior. But she was sad because she was never going to bare Northern Warrior's children. However, knowing she could enjoy his love any time, any place more than made up for that loss!

Before the next moon, Northern Warrior made her a Spirit Shield, tomahawk, and knife. They rode out with three horses each and robes, weapons, and utensils. No food or water was taken. Bear Hunter knew his daughter was now a Vampire and would remain sixteen, young, beautiful, and in love with her husband for all eternity. It scared him to have that knowledge as he and his wife would grow old and die. Never seeing any grandchildren from Morning Star.

Chapter 9

The Children Continued

Eastern Star

Two months after Northern Warrior left, Eastern Star went on her Vision Quest. She Who Speaks to the People came and told her the same vision as Northern Warrior. Only Eastern Star was told that she would marry a White Man, Cody Roberts. She and her sister would be a bridge between the People and the White Man. It would also gain access to more demons and avenues to find the Portals.

For two years, Eastern Star bided her time. Training and training to find and kill demons. On September 9, 1863, Eastern Star set out on her own. She was as tall as I was. She was beautiful with long flowing black hair to the middle of her back. She wore an eagle feather in her hair pointing to the East. She was more breasted than I was and as voluptuous as me!

When Eastern Star left, her face was painted white with red around her eyes. She wore a loin cloth and the tight deerskin on her top. She rode a white or gray horse, followed by two horses of the same color. She carried a shield, tomahawk, and bow strapped to her back. She had knives on either side of her hips. And her coup stick, and quiver of arrows were on her horse. She rode alone with Dante and Markus walking on either side of her.

From time to time, she ran into travelers. Men drooled after her, making sexual remarks. They wanted her and talked of ravaging her. She would smile and show them blood red eyes and her fangs. It usually deterred any further comments. The very few that did not heed her warning were left dead on the side of the road. All their blood drained from them.

The farther East, she traveled the more Whites she saw. She couldn't even count their numbers. It was then, Eastern Star was in St. Louis, that she realized she would eventually have to change the style of clothes that she wore and the way she would have to wear her hair. But never her eagle feather. She decided to return to our

Village and discuss this with me. She headed back west in April 1864!

In May 1864, Easter Star rode into Fort Laramie. She had no paint on and she rode in with confidence. She noticed two demons with obsidian eyes watching her. They were White Men! She saw their lust for her and a desire to kill her. She rode to the far end of the fort and dismounted. They walked toward her!

"Well, Clem, looky what we have here. A right pretty squaw. Bet she has a tight pussy! We need to see just how tight it is! Right, Clem?"

"Yeah! She looks downright ripe to me!"

Eastern Star had tied her horses to a hitching post and never said a word to them. She needed to get them off the street. No one would see how she would kill them! She walked into the alley off where she had tied her horses. Clem and his friend followed her!

"Hey, we're talking to you, bitch! We want your pussy whether you give it to us peaceful like or we take it!"

She was about to show them her eyes and fangs! But she heard a voice behind them at the entrance of the alley!

"Miss, are these scrum bags bothering you?"

She looked up and a tall, slim but muscular White Man with hair as yellow as a Texas Yellow Rose and blue eyes looked at her. She bit her lower lip. Was this Cody Roberts? Hope so because Eastern Star wanted him!

The men had taken out their guns and were pointing them at him. He had been distracted by the beautiful maiden he saw in the alley. She was breath taking.

"Son, if I were you, I would mosey on down the road if you want to live another day! Understand? Real men are here to take care of that woman!"

The young man smiled. He drew so fast that neither of the men saw it. Eastern Star did! He shot the guns out of their hands.

"You are the ones who need to mosey! Now, get!"

"Son, do you really think you can kill us with those pea shooters?"

"No, but I can!"

It was Eastern Star, and she sank her fangs into the one who had talked to Clem! She drank his

blood. The young man just stood there watching what that woman was doing!

"Vampire! God help us!"

As Eastern Star drained all the man's blood, she looked at Clem. How could he call on a God when he was a demon? White Men never ceased to amaze her. Clem started to run but he ran right into the gun of the young man. The young man pulled back the hammer! "'Going someplace? If what you said is true and I can't kill you! I bet I could slow you down a mite!"

Eastern Star had thrown the other man's body down and it turned to dust. She came up behind Clem who was terrified!

"Time for you to die, Clem!"

She sank her fangs into Clem. She started drinking his blood. But Eastern Star's eyes were rivetted on the young man. She had to find out who he was. He smiled at her! He was not scared of her in the least. He winked at her and holstered his gun and stood there waiting for her. She almost smiled as she drained Clem's blood. The young man took off his bandana and walked over to the horse trough and soaked it. By now Clem was dead, on the ground, and he turned to dust. The lower portion of her mouth was covered in blood. He handed her the wet cloth!

"Here to wash your face with! You are one right pretty woman. Remind me to never get on your bad side! I'm Cody Roberts!"

She was wiping her mouth clean! Until she heard his name. It was him! He was the one she was destined to be with. About that time, Dante and Markus strolled up behind her. Cody noticed the wolves!

"Ah, friends of yours?"

Eastern Star talked to the wolves!

"Dante and Markus, this Cody Roberts!"

They recognized the name and sat!

"Yes, this is Dante and that is Markus. They are my protectors!"

"From what? Yourself?"

That made Eastern Star laugh!

"Cody, I am Eastern Star! By now you know I am a Spirit Warrior, a Vampire!"

"Get that! But I thought Vampires only roamed at night? The sunlight burned them!"

"That is true! But I have the power of the wolves and of the Vampire! I can travel in the daylight or the night! I think I am called a hybrid! Part Vampire, part wolf!"

"Makes you very tempting!"

"Cody, my real protector told me of you. That it is foretold that you will become my Mate. My husband! I will be your wife. Does that scare you knowing if that happens, you will be turned like me?"

"Nah! Sound kind of amazing! Besides, who could turn down a beautiful maiden as yourself with a body to die for!"

That made her smile! She looked at him very seductively!

"Cody? Do you want my, what did he call it? My pussy?"

"More than anything on this planet! As long as I get you with it!"

She pulled him behind a shed! They were against a wall. Eastern Star looked around and she stripped off her loin cloth. She unbuttoned his pants and pulled out his manhood. Right there against that wall, Cody took Eastern Star's virginity. It did not take very long for them to call their names! She kissed him and looked into his eyes!

"I love you, Cody Roberts! And in the sight of Maheo, we are husband and wife. You may mate with your wife again, if you would like?"

"I would but we need to be married by a preacher. Then, I will mate with you again and again and again!"

They found the Chaplin of the Fort. He was reluctant to marry them, but Cody and his gun persuaded him to do so. They were married! Cody checked them into the only hotel at the Fort. They spent the night making love until a few hours before dawn. That is when Eastern Star turned Cody. By daybreak, Cody was a Vampire.

After she turned Cody, Eastern Star told him they were going to need to change the type of clothes they wore, their manners, and the way she wore her hair. Eastern Star had a lot of money she had taken from demons she killed. They traveled eastward and at Denver Eastern Star purchased dresses, undergarments, and shoes. It took her a while to get use to them but decided to wear her

hair up and under hats that she bought. Always with an eagle feather in them pointing to the right.

She bought Cody suits and boots! They traveled back to St. Louis. Cody was a well-mannered man and he taught Eastern Star those manners. He had grown up in Philadelphia Society but ran away at sixteen to the West and learned how to use a gun. In St. Louis, they booked passage on a Steamboat and spent years traveling up and down the Mississippi River looking for the portal of the demons. Cody became very good at poker and became a gambler with

Eastern Star at his side. She scanned for demons to seduce and kill! She only slept with her husband, Cody!

Chapter 10

The Children Continued

Southern Warrior

In October 1863, Southern Warrior went on his Vision Quest. His Father put skewers in his back and with sinew tethers, he attached Buffalo skulls that Southern Warrior drug for three days before falling into a trance. The tethers never broke! She Who Speaks to the People gave him the same instructions as Northern Warrior and Eastern Star. She told Southern Warrior that he would travel down into the very southern tip of Texas to a place called Brownsville. He would cross the border into Mexico. There he would find his Mate, Juanita Suarez! She would speak no English, but he would understand her language, Spanish! She would be very beautiful but a full head shorter than him. Coming up to his chest. She would be heavier than I was but have breasts and a body more voluptuous that mine. She would love him with all of heart and body.

Southern Warrior waited and on September 19, 1865, he painted his face yellow with green around his eyes! He was the New Beginning, the Southern Spirit Warrior! He mounted a black mare and led two other black mares and rode out of our Village. He had his weapons, robes, and other utensils with him. Raul and Apollo walked beside his horse. He headed south and traveled for

two years, searching for Juanita and demons.

In August, 1867, Southern Warrior rode into Matamoros, Mexico. Raul and Apollo walked beside him. Many people ran from the sight of Southern Warrior and his wolves. He came to a Cantina and hotel. He was going to get a room, take a bath, and have a beer. Southern Warrior liked the taste of beer but not whiskey. He did not like the way it made him feel. He lost control of his Vampire self when he drank whiskey. He had gold coins that he had taken off a demon he killed in El Paso.

"Room and a bath!"

The clerk looked at Southern Warrior!

"Have money?"

Southern Warrior slapped a twenty-dollar gold coin down. The clerk's eyes got big!

"That will get you a room and bath for a month here, Amigo!"

"Good! I stay here for a month! Bath once a week! Will the rest get me beer every day?"

"Yes, sir!"

Southern Warrior went and got his things! He told Raul and Apollo to stay in the alley way! He would find meat for them. He saw a café across the street and went there!

"Do you have steak?"

"See, Senior!"

He pulled out a ten-dollar gold piece!

66

"Will this buy me four large uncooked steaks?"

"See!"

The owner got Southern Warrior what he wanted. He took them to the wolves and gave each of them two steaks. They were hungry and started eating them. Southern Warrior went into the hotel and the clerk gave him a key and a towel.

"Bath house is out back!"

Southern Warrior went upstairs and put all his things inside the room. He pulled out a clean shirt and buckskin pants and went down the back stairs to the bath house. It was there that he saw two men with obsidian eyes forcing a young Hispanic girl into a corner. They had lust in their eyes!

"Come on girl! All we want is a poke each! You can take us both on!"

They spoke in Spanish and Southern Warrior understood every word. The girl struggled and protested!

"I am not a whore! I am a virgin! Leave me alone!"

"Even better! Been a long time since I poked a virgin! Right, Jesus?"

"Too long, Antonio!"

"Gentlemen, you heard the lady! She wants to be left alone! Leave! Unless you want to feel my fury!"

The demons turned to Southern Warrior. His eyes turned red, and he showed them his fangs.

Even the girl saw them and was frightened.

"We were only funnin'! We weren't going to hurt her!"

Jesus drew his gun and fired at Southern Warrior!"

"Take that Vampire! Silver bullet through the heart!"

Southern Warrior looked at the hole in his shirt! Silver did not harm him!

"See, you just ruined a perfectly good buckskin shirt. Now I am going to have to patch it. But not before I kill you, Jesus!"

Southern Warrior was in front of Jesus in a second and sank his fangs into his neck. He drank all of Jesus' blood. Antonio and the girl watched in horror as Southern Warrior killed Jesus. When he finished with Jesus, Southern Warrior wiped the blood off with Jesus' shirt. The minute before Jesus turned to dust. He turned to Antonio!

"If I, were you, I would run. Unless you want to end up like your friend!"

"That was my brother, Vampire!"

Antonio drew his gun and unloaded his six-shooter full of silver bullets into Southern Warrior! Southern Warrior looked in disgust at his shirt! It was now full of bullet holes around his heart area!

"Now it is really ruined! I warned you, Antonio!"

Southern Warrior was behind Antonio so fast, neither he nor the girl believed it. Southern Warrior took all of Antonio's blood and wiped off his mouth with his shirt and tossed Antonio's dead body aside! He looked at the girl! She was terrified!

"It's alright, I will not hurt you! You can leave now! You are safe! By the way, I am Southern Warrior. I am sure you know I am a Vampire!"

The girl was starting to calm. She looked at him and started to cry! Southern Warrior took her into his arms and comforted her. She gained some composure!

"My name is Juanita Suarez! Banditos killed my parents two weeks ago. I watched from the place my parents made me hide. There was nothing I could do. I have no place to go. I have not eaten in two days! Thank you for helping me. But I am afraid, I will have to become a prostitute in order to survive!"

Southern Warrior took two twenty-dollar god coins out and gave them to her!

"Go get a room and something to eat. Tomorrow, I will give you a horse to travel to another place so you can find family and start a new life!"

She refused to take the coins. She shook her head no! She looked into his eyes!

"I know I am supposed to be with you! I can feel it! I am Aztec! You are the one! You are my Mate! You are to make me a Vampire. I am your woman! Come let us take a bath together and start our lives together!"

Juanita took Southern Warrior into the bath house. A hot bath had already been drawn. She shed her clothes and Southern Warrior did the same. They got into the tub. He was not gentle with Juanita at first. And then, he made sweet, soft love to her. She called his name so softly. He

called hers. She smiled at him and gave a tender kiss!

"It appears Southern Warrior, we are a couple now and will be for the rest of our lives. Please make love to me again. Then, turn me, My Lover!"

They made love again. She was his now and until the end of time. She laid against the tub, waiting for him! Southern Warrior was trying to determine an area where no one could detect his bite for turning her. He saw her inner thigh next to her pussy. He went down on her. She screamed his name. He bit into her leg at the femoral and sucked her blood just to the point of death.

Everything was black! She awoke, gasping for air with lungs that really did not fill! She was undead. The illusion of breathing and a beating heart. Her eyes were red, she was hungry for blood. Southern Warrior slit his wrist and offered it to her. She drank and drank. It was sweet and the blood gave her power. Southern Warrior pulled her mouth form his wrist!

"Enough, Juanita!"

She sat there soaking in her new powers. Hearing everything. Feeling every movement of the earth. Seeing for miles. She was on top of the world. She was insatiable for him. All she wanted right now was that hard penis Southern Warrior always had for her. He could have her any way and any time he wanted. She was so in love with him. After a week, her desire for him tempered. Just a little but enough for Southern Warrior to start planning with the wolves their next moves.

"Juanita? Why did the banditos kill your parents? Who are they?"

Juanita told the story of her parents. Her father grew agave and made Tequila for the area Cantinas.

He and her mother made enough money for a comfortable life. But a Bandito name, Poncho Herrera, started raiding and buying up agave farms from the local farmers. If you did not accept his ridiculous low offer, he simply killed the whole family. Her Father would not accept the offer and Poncho had killed her father and mother.

Southern Warrior sat there soaking in her story! He looked at Juanita!

"Well, it sounds like we need to make a visit to Poncho Herrera!"

"Southern Warrior, he has fifty to sixty banditos with him. They would tear you apart!"

"No, Poncho sounds like a demon and we need to find out how many demons are riding with him!"

The next morning, they mounted their horses and rode for three days to the Hacienda where Poncho Herrera headquartered. Southern Warrior estimated about sixty banditos. Now he scoured their faces. He taught Juanita what to look for. Obsidian eyes! In total there were twelve demons and when Poncho stepped on the front porch. Thirteen!

"The wolves say that once we start killing demons, the rest will scatter! Juanita, we have to lure the demons into the hills. You may have to seduce them but not sleep with them. I know this will be

hard, but you have to do it to avenge your mother and father!"

Juanita thought about it, a while. She looked Southern Warrior!

"No, I will do it for you, my love! I don't have to sleep with them?"

"No!"

"Only, maybe touch them?"

"Yes!"

"Do I have to do them orally?"

"Only if you want to!"

"Do I have to let them touch my pussy?"

"Again, only if you want to!"

"Touching only, Southern Warrior! No kissing! My kisses, my

pussy, and my mouth are only for you! Do you understand, my

Love?"

"Yes!"

"If they try those things with me, you must kill them before it

happens! I could not live with myself if they violated me! I couldn't

live with you because I would feel I betrayed you!"

There were tears in her eyes. Southern Warrior knew this was very

hard for her to get her head around. He touched her face, and she cradled her face and his hand with her hand. The tears disappeared. She was happy again. He smiled at her!

"My Lover, take my breath away! Make me always remember who I belong to! Make me remember who I am in love with! My Spirit Warrior!"

He took her breath away and she was happy. He lay with her in the hills. He knew starting in a few days they would have to watch the demons. Learn their routines and routes. That would take several days. From there the wolves would formulate a plan.

The next morning, they rode back to Matamoros. Southern Warrior gathered his possessions from the hotel. He told the Clerk to keep the rest of the money for himself. The Clerk was very happy that meant sixteen American dollars for him.

Since they needed no food or water, they rode out of Matamoros at night. They traveled night and day. When they found grass and water, they stopped for the horses to rest. They had bought several sacks of Oats for the horses to eat and feeding sacks to hang on them to feed. They had taken six horses with them. It took only two days to get back to Herrera's Hacienda. They camped in the hills about five miles from the headquarters!

The Hacienda had belonged to Pedro and Rita Sanchez and their three children. The Sanchez's had been the largest of nine Agave farms that Poncho had taken over. The house was huge and sprawling. It had a huge front porch, and it was located next to a bubbling stream. The way it sat you could see for miles. Very defendable but not against the numbers of Poncho's army. When Pedro refused to sell to Poncho, they killed Pedro and his only son, Jose! Rita and her two teenage daughters were given over to Poncho's men. They locked them in the Master Bedroom, and many said they would return for their sexual pleasure with each and every one of them.

It became very apparent to Rita that Poncho's men were going to rape each of them and continue to do so for a very long time. Rita could endure it, but she knew her daughters could not. Rita had a gun hidden under the mattress. She told the girls to sit on the bed and to forgive her for she and their father loved them very much. She could not see them suffer what those men would do to them. They forgave her and with tears in her eyes, she put a bullet in each of their heads. As

Poncho's men broke down the door and rushed in, a crying Rita placed the barrel of the gun in her mouth and pulled the trigger!

That was the story, Juanita and Southern Warrior heard from many of Poncho's men in the Cantina in the nearby Village. They would go there to drink tequila and listen to Poncho's men boast about their kills and how they wished they could have felt those females' pussies. Southern Warrior had to calm down Juanita each time they told the story. Her eyes would turn red, and her fangs would show.

She could not take it anymore and lured two of Poncho's demons into the alley when Southern Warrior was not paying attention. She leaned against a wall, looking very seductively at them!

"Want my pussy? I think I could take you both on at once. May be one could have my pussy and one could have my mouth!"

One of the demons started kissing her neck and moving her skirt up with his hand. She appeared to enjoy it and just has his hand got to her vagina she sank her fangs into his neck. She drank and drank! The other demon screamed and turned to run. He ran right into Southern Warrior with red eyes and fangs. Two demons were drained of their blood. Two demons were now dust! Now there were eleven!

Juanita and Southern Warrior had been in the Cantina for a week. But it was now getting too dangerous there. Too many of Poncho's men frequented this Saloon. They got away with their killing this one time. But once the demons' clothing and dust were found, the men would be on alert. They could not dispose of the clothes because after killing the demons, two of Poncho's

drunk men started down the alley to relieve themselves. Juanita and Southern Warrior disappeared into the shadows and the men found the clothes and dust. They alerted all of the men in the Cantina, and they searched the alley for the killer(s). But Juanita and Southern Warrior were long gone, heading for their camp, five miles from Poncho's Hacienda.

They found a valley surrounded by cliffs within the hills about a mile further down the road. It was hidden and you entered it through a corridor, cliff walls on either side. It went for about fifty feet and was big enough to lead a horse down. About halfway down, there was a crevice wide and deep enough for a man to hide. When you came out of the corridor there was a large valley with lots of green grass for about ten horses. On the other side of the cliff walls was a much larger corridor, big enough to ride out of, leading horses. There was a clearing just off the smaller corridor. It was perfect!

From that base camp, they watched Poncho's demons and men. For three weeks they watched. What they learned was Poncho was not much of a strategist. Every evening at six, two of his demon commanders would ride down the road to the Cantina. About an hour later, a group of men appeared and rode to the Cantina, as well. It was like clockwork, every day! A different commander duo and their soldiers they commanded went to the saloon. This was going to be so easy. But Southern Warrior knew they could probably only accomplish this, two or three times. After that, Poncho would be left with only four or five commanders, and he would hole up with them and the rest of the men to protect Poncho!

The wolves came up with a plan. It was very simple. A little before six, Juanita would go down by the road and gather stones and deadwood in her dress. She would pull her dress up to make a basket, exposing her bare bush. When the demons spotted her, she was to stand there, looking seductive. She was to make a sexual remark to them, drop what she was loading and run up the hill. At the top, she was to raise her dress, showing her bare ass and make another sexual remark. When they started up the hill, she was to run to the mouth of the corridor and wait. As they topped the hill and started down it, she would tell them she had a soft bed inside to take care of each of them. She would disappear into the corridor, running to the end. When they entered the corridor, Juanita was to keep talking to them making sexual remarks, so they followed her voice. Southern Warrior would let the first one by the crevice and as the second passed his hiding place, Southern Warrior would step out and take the demon's blood. As the first one turned around to see what was happening to his companion, Juanita would take that demon's blood.

When the demons were dead and turned to dust, Southern Warrior would build a fire and burn the demons' clothing. Then, he would tend to the horses. Juanita would take Evergreen branches from inside the valley and follow Southern Warrior. As he led the horses into the corridor, Juanita would brush the tracks, smoothing from the road to the corridor. Southern Warrior would unsaddle the horses and throw the saddles and saddle bags into the treed area of the valley. He would burn the saddle blanket and contents of the saddle bags, keeping any money or gold he found. Juanita would brush out the dust piles and from the road to inside the corridor no one would know that any one was camped there. This would all be accomplished before the next group of men went down the road. The wolves' plan worked to perfection.

The next evening when the first demon duo came, Juanita was showing her bush. When they got within a hundred feet of her, Juanita looked at them.

"See something you like and want? Come and get it!"

And she giggled, dropped what he was gathering, and ran up the hill. At the top, she lifted her dress, showing her bare ass!

"I need real men! Think you can handle this ass?"

They were already coming up the hill. Juanita giggled again and ran down the hill to the mouth of the corridor. They were now at the top of the hill. She lifted her dress, showing her bare ass again.

"Amigos, hurry! I have a soft bed inside. I am very wet between my legs. I need a hard manhood now, not later. I will satisfy both of you!"

She turned and went inside the corridor and ran to the other side and waited. She heard them laughing and talking about what they were going to do to her. Probably multiple times. Juanita was smiling!

The trap was set! Now the cheese needed to be put on the trap! She shed her dress and stood naked at the other side. When they got to the mouth of the corridor, they saw her naked body, her luscious large breasts!

"I need to be ravaged! It is the only way you will give me sexual pleasure. Come, fuck my brains out!"

And she turned and walked away. They could not run but they walked very fast. One followed the other. They were chuckling. The first one passed the crevice, then, the second one passed. Southern Warrior stepped from his hiding place. He grabbed the second demon's shoulder and sank his fangs into that demon's neck. The first demon stopped and turned to see what the commotion was. Southern Warrior's eyes met the first demon's eyes. The demon went to pull his gun, but a naked Juanita was there behind him, sinking her fangs into his neck. Southern Warrior and Juanita were drinking blood and soon killed both demons. When both were dead, Juanita looked at Southern Warrior. She wanted him and she wanted him now! She went to him and pulled him against her, against the cliff walls!

"Juanita, we do not have time for this right now!"

"Sure, we do! We have plenty of time! Ravage me, My Lover! I have never wanted you as badly as I want you now!"

She ripped off his loin cloth. She turned around, offering herself to him from behind!

"Ravage me like you have never ravaged me before, Lover Boy!"

Southern Warrior ravaged her! He made her call his name three times before he called hers. It was the best sex they had ever had together!

"Juanita, we have to get started!"

Juanita already had an Evergreen branch and she followed Southern Warrior naked. The horses were led, and their tracks swept away. He looked back at Juanita's naked body. She looked at Southern Warrior and smiled. She saw his want and his desire for her! This was going to be a long sexual night for them. That made her giggle! What had to be burned was burned. Saddles and saddle bags were hidden. Dust was swept clean! The horses were released out the other side of the valley. And the sex began. Soft, gentle, and loving sex all night long!

The horses returned to the Hacienda. The first group of men said Juan and Pedro never came to the Cantina. Poncho was suspicious but let another group go the next evening. Miguel and Benito's horses returned but not their riders. Now Poncho was angry. The next evening, he sent Tonto and Alonso out first. Fifteen minutes later, Poncho sent twenty riders out following them.

Southern Warrior knew this time would be very dangerous. But he wanted to send Poncho a message. Just before six, he and Juanita went down to the road. A little, ways up the road was a tree off the road. It was there that Southern Warrior removed his loin cloth and sat with his back against the tree. Juanita raised her dress and straddled him. Inserting him into her and she exposed a nibble for him. They had just finished calling each other's name when Tonto and Alonso rode up!

"Amigo, can we have some?"

Juanita got off Southern Warrior. She really did not want to she was savoring that to die for orgasm he had given her. But she looked at the demons very seductively! Southern Warrior looked at the demons!

"Of course, you fuck her while your companion and I watch!"

They dismounted and Tonto went to the tree and removed his pants, exposing a somewhat hard manhood to her. Limp dick! Southern Warrior and Alonso watched!

"Amigo, you are not hard enough for me yet! I must make you harder so I can enjoy the fuck!"

Juanita straddled Tonto and exposed her breasts to him. She wrapped her hand around his limp penis. It so disgusted her. He was sucking on a nibble, and he wanted to poke her. She looked into his eyes. They turned red and her fangs appeared. She sank them into Tonto's neck and drank. Alonso realized what was happening, but Southern Warrior sank his fangs into Alonso and drained his blood! When both were dead, they laid their bodies alongside the road. They turned to dust. Juanita and Southern Warrior went to the top of the hill and waited. Soon, twenty riders appeared. As they approached, they saw the riderless horses and the piles of dust with Tonto and Alonso's clothes on top of the dust piles. Juanita and Southern Warrior appeared at the top of the hill! He looked at the riders!

"Tell, Poncho we are coming for the rest of his commanders and him. Tell him to count the remaining hours of his life!"

The sun was starting to set. Southern Warrior and Juanita's eyes turned right red! They showed the riders their fangs! The riders turned and ran back to the Hacienda. There they gave Poncho the message! Poncho needed a plan, or he was dead!

But Southern Warrior and Juanita did not give him time to think. That very night and the next night, the wolves stole into the headquarters and killed the remaining commander demons. All that was left was Poncho. Southern Warrior and Juanita bided their time. They knew Poncho's days were numbered!

Over the next few days, Poncho's riders began disappearing. They were human! None were smart enough to run the Agave and Tequila Operation. By the fifth day, only six of the most loyal humans remained with Poncho.

Juanita knew the Sanchez Hacienda. She had played with the Sanchez daughters as they all grew up. Juanita was a year older than the oldest Sanchez girl and three years older than the youngest. She knew there were corridors between the Hacienda outer and inner walls. Hiding places. One hiding place was to the Study where Poncho was holed up in. His loyal followers were patrolling outside the Study of the house. Juanita knew that just outside the barn was an entrance to a tunnel that went from the barn to the Study's hiding place. It was an escape route.

Juanita and Southern Warrior entered the tunnel. It had not been used in years. Pedro had probably forgotten about it! They followed it and it opened into a corridor around the Study. Once inside the corridor, there were places where one could look into the Study. Poncho was sitting at the desk, drinking tequila. He did not know that the door into the Study from the corridor was right behind him. Juanita walked to the door and found the latch on her side. It was unlocked! She took a breath and flung the door open! Poncho came up with his gun and Juanita pressed her belly against the barrel. Poncho fired six times, six silver bullets into her body. She smiled at him, not even dazed by the bullets.

"This is for my mother!"

She sank her fangs into a startled Poncho and drank half his blood!

"And this is for my father!"

She drank the rest of his blood. She dragged his lifeless body to the door of the Study. She opened it and threw his body past the two guards on either side of the door. She slammed the door shut and locked it. She and Southern Warrior waited for the humans! They never came!

When the humans saw Poncho's dead body and saw it turn to dust! They all ran for the hills!

Juanita and Southern Warrior heard horses galloping away from the Hacienda. They walked out of the Study and found they were alone! The next day, they rode for Matamoros. There at the Mexican Land Office, Juanita laid claim to the Sanchez property and the other nine Agave properties. She paid the brides to accomplish it and paid the fees for the land claims. She used the money they found in the Study in a strong box! Gold, lots of it!

She paid to have the nine houses torn down, including her parents' house. It saddened her but she could not bear looking at the place where they died. Where the house and outbuildings had been torn down, she planted Agave. In all their acreage was over two thousand acres. All but ten acres around the Hacienda were Agave plants.

They kept two acres around the Hacienda for the house. They built a fortress around it. The remaining eight acres they turned into a Tequila Plant. It had its own fortress around it. Within a few years, they were producing enough Tequila to supply saloons and tavern in Northern Mexico and in the United States. From Los Angeles to the Carolinas.

The Tequila they sold was called Jose's Gold. It was named after the Sanchez's dead son! It made Juanita and Southern Warrior very rich. The Hacienda was their base headquarters of the Corporation they formed in 1880.

In order for Southern Warrior and Juanita to fit into high society, he had to teach Juanita to dress, talk, and be a lady. Southern Warrior taught her English and worked on her diction. He spent the

better part of a year, grooming her. Southern Warrior had learned from his visits to Eastern Star and Cody about manners and dress. He worked on her language and manners. By 1871, no one would ever have known Juanita had been a Mexican Aztec. She had poise, diction, and class. But in bed, she was Juanita! Southern Warrior's lover!

In 1872, Southern Warrior took Juanita and twenty thousand dollars in gold to New Orleans. There he bought her under garments, dresses of all kinds, shoes to match, furs, coats, and hats to match. She looked every bit of the lady she was. He bought himself suits, custom made shirts, socks, shoes, coats, and derby hats. Together they were the most well-dressed couple in New Orleans. They secretly got married and became known as New Orleans' Sweethearts!

In that same year with a two hundred-thousand-dollar bank draft, they bought a mansion in the high society district of Dallas, Texas. They had several hundred-thousands of dollars transferred to a Dallas bank. Poncho's strong box held over six-hundred-thousand-dollars in gold. The Tequila Factory by now was bringing in millions.

They had their new house redecorated with wallpaper and new furniture. They moved in on January 3, 1873. Life was good! They were rich! And they threw a lavish party, opening their home to all the Dallas-Ft. Worth area. The party cost them sixty-thousand-dollars, worth of food, drink, party favors, and security. It was worth every penny! Even though they were Cheyenne and Aztec Hispanic, they were accepted by the area socialites. Juanita went by her middle name, Rochelle! Southern Warrior changed his name to Rick! They were known has Rick and Rochelle Cuervo, makers of Jose's Gold!

Chapter 11

The Children Continued

Western Warrior

In November 1865, Western Star ventured to the sacred cave. There she had her Vision. She Who Speaks to the People gave her instructions as she was told the same as her siblings. She told Western Star that she would be taking Rudolph and Brutus with her when she left on her eighteenth birthday to find the Western Portal.

"Tell, your mother that when you leave, two wolves will appear to replace the eight that have gone with her children. One will be a white male called the Seventh Son and one will be a black female name Sacred Wolf. The Seventh Son will join She Wolf as your mother's protectors. Sacred Wolf will join He Wolf as your Father's protectors. These wolves will have special powers to see demons before you and your family do. They will teach She Wolf and He

Wolf to see as they do. Turning their eyes red whenever a demon is around because there are many that are coming!"

She Who Speaks to the People told Western Star that she would meet her Mate in the Indian Territory not long after she left her Village. He would be a bounty hunter. Very tall, very muscular! With a stubble beard, short black hair, brown eyes, and black skin. He would be riding a black gelding with silver on his saddle and bridle. He would be wearing two Pearl-handled guns. His name will be Douglas Glover. Western Star was to love him, mate with him, and turn him. They were to ride the Western parts of America, killing demons, looking for the Western Portal.

Western Star awoke and left the sacred cave. When she got to the bottom of the mountain, she heard a rumbling, and she looked up. The mouth of the cave was now sealed with rocks. Western Star was the last of my children to seek a Vision. I assumed She Who Speaks to the People sealed the sacred cave as there was no longer a use for it. Sealed away from the People. But more importantly, sealed away from the coming Whites.

Western Star told me and her Father of her Vision. She told us of the coming wolves. She told us of her future husband. Then, she told me of the sacred cave's sealing! I was very sad because that cave was very sacred to me. My Vision Quest and my children's Quests. The meeting of She Wolf and the eight gray wolves. I knew I would see She Who Speaks to the People through dreams, but the sacred cave was special to me. It was the place my father showed me.

On September 12, 1867, Western Star painted her face red with black around her eyes. She was the setting sun, the Western Spirit Warrior. She rode a bay horse, leading two other bay horses. She carried her shield, tomahawk, and bow on her back. She had her Coup Stick and a quiver of arrows on her horse. The two horses behind her carried robes and utensils she would need. On her hips were her knives.

Western Star was tall, almost as tall as her grandfather. Her body was even more voluptuous than

mine. She had very large breasts and she wore a loin cloth with a special made buckskin top that tied around her neck and around just below her breasts. The top opened past the beginning of her breasts and men drooled at the sight of her. What did the White Man call it? Cleavage! Western Star flaunted her large breasts. I guess I could not blame her. She was gorgeous and desirable. She took Rudolph and Brutus with her.

The one thing I noticed about all my children was they left looking eighteen. When I saw them again, they were still eighteen, forever! They had turned at sixteen and again at eighteen. No matter what, they were very handsome or beautiful. Young! And the Spirit Warriors they had become.

Two days after Western Star left, black and white wolves appeared in the Village. They walked straight to our lodge. I greeted them!

"You must be The Seventh Son?"

"At your service!"

"And you must be Sacred Wolf?"

"Yes, I am!"

The Seventh Son joined She Wolf and whispered in her ear. She Wolf's eyes turned red. Sacred Wolf did the same to He Wolf and his eyes turned red!

Lone Wolf and I waited for a sign from She Who Speaks to the People for our next mission after Western Star left. But this was Western Star's time, and I knew she was in search of the man who would become her husband.

In January 1868, Western Star was riding on a road in Indian Territory. She had run into several men on the road. Since she was covered by a Buffalo Robe most did not take notice of her. Especially when she flashed red eyes and sharp fangs at those who did look!

On an unusually warm afternoon, Western Star stopped and dismounted. She shed her Buffalo Robe and wet a cloth to rinse the sweat from her face and neck. Two White Men with obsidian eyes stopped by her horses.

"My, oh, my! Just look at you Squaw! I bet you could poke with the best of them. Why don't we go over into the bushes, and you give me one fine poke! Then, you can give Jerry, here, a poke! What do you say, pretty little lady?"

Western Star looked at them with disgust! She thought about seducing them and killing them. But they looked way to slimy to touch!

"I don't poke, scum!"

"Who are you calling scum? I have a mind to take you right here on the road. Ravage you many times!"

"You and what army?"

"Why you little bitch!"

Jerry drew his pistol!

"Now, Squaw, strip and spread them pretty legs while Shorty fucks you!"

Western Star took off her shield and put it on the ground. She was going to put her silver bladed knife into Jerry's chest once she took her knives off her body. But she heard a voice!

"Miss, are these two scumbags bothering you?"

"Nothing I can't handle, Mr.?"

"Douglas Glover at your service, Miss?"

"Western Star!"

The demons recognized her name and Jerry holstered his pistol!

"I apologize, Western Star. I did not know it was you! We will be on our way. Good afternoon!"

"Not so fast, Jerry and Shorty! You started this with me. I am going to finish this!"

Before Jerry could say anything, Western Star had jumped on his horse's back and sank her fangs into Jerry. The horse reared and stayed that way for a little while. When it came down, Jerry's blood had all been drained. She tossed his body onto the ground.

Shorty tried to leave, but he heard a gun click!

"Stay where you are, Shorty McGinnis! You have a bounty on your head!"

But Western Star pulled Shorty off his horse and drained all his blood. She let his body hit the ground. She cleaned her face with Shorty's shirt tail!

"Sorry, Spirit Warrior! They were demons and needed to die!"

Shorty and Jerry's bodies turned to dust!

"And there goes my bounty!"

"Sorry! I would like to make it up to you if you are interested?"

"What were you thinking of beautiful lady?"

"Give you my body if you want it?"

"Lady, there isn't a man on this planet that wouldn't want your body. You're not a whore, are you?"

"You would be my first time and I could easily be your last! We could ride together, and you could have me any time you wanted!"

"Miss that is mighty tempting!"

Douglas looked at a very seductive Western Star! He shrugged his shoulders!

"Why not! That body could make me yours forever!"

"That's the plan, Douglas! Shall we in the bushes?"

Western Star removed her top and loin cloth and laid them on her horse walking naked into the bushes. Douglas followed her! He found her lying on her back with her legs spread for him. He removed his clothes. Western Star looked at his very hard, large penis and smiled. She was going to so enjoy that enormous penis inside her multiple times!

"Douglas, you cannot be gentile with me. It's my first time! Understand?"

Douglas got between her legs and thrust hard inside her. Praise Maheo! That thrust popped her virtue fast and the sheer pleasure reined over her body. By the time Douglas cried out, Western Star had screamed his name three times. She was breathing hard!

"Douglas again! I think I just fell in love with you and that huge manhood of yours. You may have to fuck my brains out at least ten times a day. Can you handle my pussy?"

Douglas laughed and got up!

"Western Star get dressed. There is a hotel a half day's ride from here. I need a soft mattress to enjoy you that may times!"

"I don't know if I can wait that long!"

"If you can't, all you have to do is ask!"

"Okay!"

And twice along the way, she did! And both times while she wrapped her arms around a tree and Douglass ravaged her from behind! Made her call his name three times each time. She fell more in love with him after each encounter.

They rode into the town and Western Star had a big smile on her face. She was remembering their last sexual experience less than an hour ago!

Douglas paid for a room for a week! He, also, paid for a bath for both. They bathed together and made love! The Clerk had given them extra towels and Douglas wrapped one around his waist. He showed Western Star how to wrap one around her body. He picked up their clothes and they went to their room. Western Star looked at Douglas seductively!

"Douglas on your back! Please? I have to show you how much I love you!"

Douglas laid on his back and Western Star took off his towel. Then, she took off hers. She went down on him. Now, traveling these past few months in the Indian Territory, she had encountered several women. Most were whores. They taught her a lot of new words. She learned new names for things. Vagina, clit, orgasm, dick, cock, penis, Blow Job, and Hand Job! A few of them let her watch them give a man a "BJ"! She learned quickly. And that is what she was doing to Douglas. He cried her name when he came in her mouth. Two other things she had learned. Came and cum! She swallowed! Western Star came up to him and kissed him. She smiled at him!

"Did you like that, my Love?"

"Oh, yes! You sure you were a virgin? When did you learn to do that?"

"A couple of whores let me watch giving men a BJ! I am a quick learner! That was my first time!"

"Well, you are most definitely an expert at it!"

That made Western Star smile even more! She snuggled against him!

"Douglas, can we talk before I make love to you again?"

Douglas laughed!

"Sweetheart, you are going to wear me out! You are insatiable!"

"You don't like it?"

"I love you so much Western Star! Screw me until I can't walk!"

"Is screwing the same as fucking?"

"Oh, yes!"

"I would so like to do that, my Love! But seriously, would you like to be a Vampire like me? I could never wear you out if you were. You would probably wear me out! Male Vampires are known to be able to do it ten times a day if given the opportunity!"

"Really! What are the other advantages?"

"You don't have to sleep or eat or drink water. You can drink whiskey or beer if you like! My brother, Southern Warrior, does that and my brother-in-law, Cody, drinks whiskey quite often. You just don't get drunk. I think you get, what do they call it?"

"A buzz?"

"That's it! You can see for miles. You can hear everything around you. And you can read people's minds. Once you become a Vampire, you will become one with the minds of the wolves. Pretty amazing!

"Everybody leaves you alone and they respect you. Because you are a Vampire with wolf powers, you can walk in the sunlight and prowl at night. And your night vision is amazing!"

"What are the disadvantages?"

"You can't eat or drink except for whiskey or beer! Of course, I was born a Vampire, so I have never eaten or drank. You drink blood! But if you drink demon blood you are good for a month. Otherwise, you drink the blood of an enemy at least once a week! In between, you drink animal blood. Deer, goat, sheep, cow! I stay away from horses and dogs!"

"What's the best part?"

"To be with me for a very long time! The only way you can die is to have your head severed from your body or have a wooden stake driven into your heart!"

"I don't know. I always enjoyed a juicy steak?"

"You mean a rare steak?"

"Yeah, with the blood juices running out! Oh, I see what you mean!"

"Cow blood is quite tasty, and you don't have to drink that much!"

"Does it hurt?"

"Not going to lie to you! You will die a human death. I did it at sixteen. It's not pleasant. Everything will go black, and you will startle awake. You will have an overwhelming need for blood! Not animal blood! My blood!"

"Where will you drink my blood from?"

"Well, I have thought about this a lot. It has to be a place no one will see. I was thinking on your inner thigh, by your man sack!"

"Seriously?"

"Yes, you have a main artery there. I could stroke your cock and give you a hand job before I drain enough blood to turn you. I could let you cum just before then. Interested?"

"Sounds delicious! Where will I drink your blood?"

Western Star spread her legs and pointed at her inner thing!

"Right here is the femoral! You can get your first nourishment there! But I will expect your tongue right here afterward!"

She was pointing at her vagina!

Douglas was smiling!

"We get to ride together? I get to be with you and only you?"

"Yes! But you need to understand we will be fighting demons! Sometimes I will have to seduce and touch them in order to kill them. But at no point will I ever have sex with them or do oral sex with them. I will not kiss them. That belongs to you and you alone. But I may have to do hand jobs! Gross!"

"If that is all you have to do, I am good with it! You ready?"

"Are you, Douglas?"

He touched her face and gave her a tender kiss! She was his!

"Western Star, I am always ready for you!"

"Then, on your back, Lover Boy!"

Western Star bit into his inner thigh and started sucking his blood. She stroked his hard penis and got faster and faster. Just before draining his blood to the point of death, Douglas called out her name! She laid back and waited!

His red eyes shot open, and he gasped for air only his lungs did not work. He looked at Western Star who was on her back. She saw his lust for blood. Western Star took a knife and slit her thigh open for him. He sank his fangs into the cut and drank the flowing blood. She grabbed his head and let him drink. It felt so good! He drank and drank!

"Douglas, darling, that's enough! Douglas, ENOUGH!"

He let go and looked at her vagina and smiled. His tongue touched her clit. She lifted her butt off the bed. What he was doing to her was driving her insane. It did not take long as she screamed with her butt off the bed! She was one satisfied female Vampire!

He got up and wiped off his face with a towel and came back to her. Kiss upon kiss upon kiss. Soon, they were making soft, sweet, gentil love to each other!

After the last lovemaking, Western Star had him lay on his back and Rudolph and Brutus came to him. They laid their heads against his. Soon, he understood their thoughts. He was now One with the wolves and was a Vampire!

A week later, they left town and roamed the Indian Territory. From time to time, they met and killed demons. They drank cow blood in between. In one of their camps, they had made love and Western Star fell asleep and She Who Speaks to the People came to her. She had a mission for

them.

"Western Star, can you hear me?"

"Yes!"

"There is a demon, his name is One-eyed Jack Ferguson. For the past two years, he has been giving poisoned Fire Water to young Warriors with maiden wives. When the Warriors die, One-eyed Jack comforts the widowed maidens, sleeps with them, and makes them with child. He has done that to as many as twenty maidens. When the babies are born, he steals them and takes them to the Western Portal to the Evil One. There they will be raised for the army of hybrid demons He is forming. You have to stop One-eyed Jack and his demons. It you don't stop him; in a hundred years he will produce enough offspring hybrids to kill all the People!"

"We will stop them!"

They rode the Indian Territory, looking for One-eyed Jack. Western Star wore the buckskin dress of a young maiden as a disguise. Towards the border of Kansas, Douglas and Western Star ran into One-eyed Jack and three of his demons. Just outside of their camp, Douglas hailed them!

"You in the camp, can we come in for some coffee?"

"Sure, come on in!"

It was One-eyed Jack! He looked at Western Star and had lust in his eye. She noticed his lust!

"Well, looky here boys! A pretty Squaw and her . . ..!"

He used the N word. She had never heard that word before and it sounded very degrading. The look on Douglas' face told her he hated that word!

"Sit a spell and have a cup of coffee!"

He poured them each a cup. They drank some! It had no taste to them. They sat and talked for a while. Then, One eyed Jack looked at Western Star!

"So, pretty Squaw? How did he get you in bed with him? Does he have something in his pants that gives you enjoyment? I've heard . . . . are huge and keep their women satisfied! That right . . ..?"

There he used the N word twice. That word was really starting to make her mad!

Hey, ...! How about a drink? Some mighty fine whiskey in the wagon! Want some, ...?"

He used that word again! I could tell Douglas was getting very angry!

"My name is Douglas, sir! Not, ...!"

"Very well, Douglas!"

One-eyed Jack said Douglas' name with a hint of displeasure. Jack went and poured a couple of cups of whiskey. Douglas and I had talked about this before entering the camp. We knew One-eyed Jack would try to poison Douglas. Douglas was immune to poison, but we had to make it look like he died! One-eyed Jack handed Douglas a cup! Douglas drained the cup!

"Want more Douglas?"

"Nah, I'm fine. Pretty good!"

"Finest sippin' Kentucky Mash! Going to sell it to the soldiers!"

Douglas started gasping for air, he foamed at the mouth. He keeled over dead! What an actor! Western Star screamed and went to him! What an actress!

"Douglas, baby? Please? My darling? He's dead! What did you give him?"

One-eyed Jack drained his cup of whiskey and smiled!

"Just whiskey! Couldn't be anything wrong with the coffee or whiskey. We both drank from the same containers!"

Western star guessed that One-eyed Jack poured something into Douglas' cup of whiskey before giving it to him! She stood there distraught. Again, what an actress!

"What am I going to do? I am all alone!"

One-eyed Jack took Western Star into his arms to comfort her!

"There, there pretty Squaw! You can come with me to the next town. I will take care of you and make sure you are safe!

"Thank you, kind sir! How will I ever repay you?"

"Oh, we can come up with some ways to repay me?"

Western Star looked aghast!

"Oh, I couldn't mate with you. Not just yet! My husband has just died. It will probably take me a few days before I could do that! But I could maybe take care of you with my hands. You know as a jester of good faith?"

"Can I touch your bare breasts?"

"I suppose that will be alright!"

"How about in my tent, now?"

"Okay!"

Western star went with One-eyed Jack and gave him a hand job while he touched her breasts. She hated every second of it. But in order to distract One-eyed Jack from what Douglas would do over the next couple of days, she gave him three to four hand jobs a day. So disgusting!

The other demons took Douglas' body and threw it into a ravine. When they left, Douglas got up and followed them back to camp.

In the middle of the night, one of the demons got up to go relieve himself. Douglas followed him and drained that demon's blood. He took the body to the ravine and threw it in. It turned to dust. Douglas crept back into the camp and took the man's blankets and saddle. He knew whose horse was whose and saddled the demon's horse. He quietly rode out toward the west.

The next morning One-eyed Jack came out of his tent. Western Star had given him another hand job. He looked around the camp. Someone was missing!

"Where's James?"

"Don't know! His stuff and horse are gone. Probably mad that he did not get some of that Squaw! We feel the same way!"

"Shut the fuck up! You know the plan! I get the Squaws!"

"Yeah, but don't seem fair! That's all we are saying!"

"Don't like it? Ride out or be killed!"

"Maybe we will?"

"Suit yourself! I need coffee! Squaw, make us coffee!"

Western Star got up and took the coffee pot over the hill and down to the stream. She started scrubbing and scrubbing her hands. She felt like his filth was all over them. She removed her top and did the same to her breasts. She had to clean herself of his scum! Douglas whistled! She ran to him and kissed him.

"Please forgive me? I had to give him hand jobs and let him touch my bare boobs. So disgusting! Please don't hate me?"

Douglass touched her face and kissed her tenderly!

"Western Star, we knew this was going to happen! Remember, just how much I love you!"

"Wish we could show each other right now?"

"Not enough time! What did they say about the missing guy?"

"That he left because One-eyed Jack wouldn't share me! The other two are pretty mad about it too! Might be an opportunity to get rid of both of them tonight. Then, I can strike in the morning!"

"Sounds like a plan!"

"Actually, Brutus came up with it!"

One-eyed Jack decided to stay camped for one more day. They would leave in the morning. Western Star guessed it was because of her hand jobs! The other two demons were getting mad at him!

That night, Douglass crept into the camp and took the blood of one of the demons while the other slept. Then, Douglas took the other one. He disposed of their bodies in the ravine. They turned to dust. He took their stuff and saddles, saddling their horses and quietly rode out. When Western Star heard Douglas ride out, she got up and started for the opening of the tent!

"Where are you going?"

"Wash my hands and relieve myself. Your load was quite large, and it is all over my hands and arms!"

"Don't taken too long!"

"Okay!"

Western Star went down to the stream and washed her hands and arms. Douglas was there. They started kissing and against a tree, they made love. It took hardly any time for them to softly call their names. Western Star went back to the tent!

"What took so long? Trying to find an escape route?"

"No! If you must know, I had to do more than pee!"

"Oh!"

"One-eyed?"

"Yes!"

"In the morning, I think I might be ready to let you touch my female part. Maybe by tomorrow night I could mate with you!"

"How about now?"

"No, in the morning!"

In the morning, Western Star woke up and One-eyed Jack was waiting for her! She removed her top and loin cloth for him! He stared to put his hand between her legs!

"Not so fast, Cowboy! I need some time to lead up to that! Take your clothes off and I will touch you and you can touch my boobs! That will get me in the mood for you to touch my female part. No kissing! I am not ready for that!"

He kissed her neck and boob! Western Star wrapped her hands around his penis and balls. Made her skin crawl. He started to more his hand down her stomach to her vagina. She struck!

She sank her fangs into One-eyed Jack's neck! Douglas walked up and watched. The surprise on One-eyed Jack's face was priceless! Western Star started drinking his blood! Halfway through sucking One-eyed Jack's blood, she stopped and looked at Douglas, smiling!

"Want to finish him off, Lover?"

"With pleasure!"

Douglas finished draining Jack's blood! He threw his body into a corner, and it turned to dust. Western Star was lusting for Douglas. She helped him strip. They made love and laid there in love again! All was good!

They kept the tent and its contents. They took the wagon and all the horses and tack. They dumped the whiskey. They took whatever they needed. Everything else would be sold. Douglas found that the wagon had a false bottom. When he pried it up, there was over fifty thousand dollars in gold and greenbacks. He put the gold in bags he found and hid them behind the seat of the wagon. He put the greenbacks in his pockets. Western Star searched and took any money out of the other demons' clothes. About a thousand dollars. Douglas confiscated all their weapons. Once done, they headed west to California!

They traveled day and night. Nations did not bother them! They entered Arizona. They met up with Eastern Star and Cody in a town called Tombstone. Eastern Star looked breath taking in her dress. She took one look at Western Star and her clothes and shook her head!

"Come on Sister, to the General Store!"

There Eastern Star bought her sister three dresses and two traveling dresses. She got Western Star under garments, stockings, and shoes for good and traveling. She, also, bought her a couple of hats! Like

Eastern Star, Western Star wore her eagle feather to the left towards the setting sun!

They spent three days with Eastern Star and Cody. They were going to stay at the hotel. When Western Star and Douglas showed up to check in, the proprietor looked at Douglas. He was a former Confederate!

"We don't give rooms to, ...!"

He used the N word! This time she could not hold back. Western Star took a twenty-dollar gold piece and slammed it on the counter!

"You will give me and my husband a room for the next three days! This should more than cover the cost of the room. Unless, of course, you want to die!"

Western Star showed the man her deep red eyes and fangs! The man peed his pants!

"Thought so! Key, please!"

They put their belongings in the room. They made love! Then, they headed to the restaurant where Eastern Star and Cody were waiting. Western Star was wearing one of the good dresses her sister had bought her. With her new under garments, she felt so much like a woman. Of course, Douglas had brought out the woman in her not less than twenty minutes ago!

They met her sister and brother-in-law for breakfast. They would eat at the restaurant for breakfast, lunch, and dinner. The food had no taste to them, but they were putting up appearances!

The day after Western Star's run in with the hotel proprietor, the City Marshall showed up at their table as they ate dinner. Clayton Matthews!

"Ma'am! May I have a word with you?"

"Certainly, Marshall! This is my sister, Eastern Star, and her husband, Cody Roberts! I am Western Star, and this is my husband, Douglas!"

"Indian?"

"Yes, my sister and I are Cheyenne!"

"Well, Western Star, the hotel proprietor says you threatened to kill him. Showed him red eyes and fangs!"

She laughed!

"Seriously, Marshall? Do I look like I have red eyes or fangs? Yes, he called my husband the N word and I don't appreciate that. I would have killed him if he used it again!"

"Understand but you can't go around threatening people. Not in my town!"

Douglas thought it was time to defuse the situation!

"Marshall, what is the name of the hotel proprietor?"

"Justin Shivers! Why?"

"You might want to look at some of your old Wanted Posters! Looks a lot like Simon Shivers, Quantrill Raiders, wanted for murder and rape!"

"I'll look into that, Mr.?"

"Glover! Douglas Glover!"

"The Bounty Hunter?"

"Yep!"

Marshal Matthews checked out his old Wanted Posters and there he was. He arrested Shivers, who was tried and found guilty. He was sentenced to hang! When they announced the sentence, Shivers just smiled. He was a demon and couldn't be hung by a mere mortal rope!

On the day of his hanging, Western Star gave the Hangman a hanging rope. He protested but she said it was a special rope that had been used on a famous outlaw. He took it! The Marshall brought out a smiling Shivers to the gallows. They put the rope around his neck and pulled the trap door lever!

Shivers was expecting to just hang there but when he reached the end of the slack, his eyes got big. He couldn't breathe! He was dying! He struggled for a few minutes and died! You see the rope that Western Star had given the Hangman was special! It was laced with silver. He turned to dust! The whole crowd was shocked!

Western Star and Douglas left for San Francisco the next day. Outside of San Francisco, they sold the wagon, extra horses, and tack. They bought a carriage and that is what they arrived in the city with. They bought a modest, upscale house. They searched for the Western Portal!

And what of the Portals? In subsequent journeys, the readers will find out they would be found, and demons killed. The Portals would be sealed. But I thought I might "wet, your appetite" as they say!

Western Star and Douglas (Wendy and Douglas) would find the first Portal in 1906 after the Great

San Francisco Earthquake. It was guarded by an evil demon called William Harris!

Eastern Star and Cody (Eve and Cody) would find the Easter Portal in Berlin, Germany in 1945. It was guarded by Adolph Heisler!

Southern Warrior and Juanita (Rick and Rochelle) would locate the Southern Portal in the Jungles of Peru in 1979. Jim Johnson was its guardian.

The final Portal, the Northern one, would be discovered by Northern Warrior and Morning Star (Nick and Sheila) in an Uranium tunnel in North Korea in 2008. It was guarded by Su Kong Moong. She was the sister of the new young North Korean Leader, Kim Kong Moong!

At Washita, the demon, General George A. Custer, would tell me the Evil One would return once all the Portals were destroyed. What was he talking about when he said the Evil One would return to earth and open new Portals everywhere? Well, the Evil One would return in 2008 and run a Giant Corporation that would provide ways for people to open billions of portals to let demons out. The Corporation? Apex!

Chapter 12

Washita

After the last of our children left the Village in 1867, Lone Wolf and I started roaming the Western part of the United States. Mainly scouting for Portals. We thought they were in America. Only one was! We killed a few demons, here and there!

While traveling, we decided to go to the new fort in Western Kansas. Fort Hays! It was the wolves that guided us there. To seek out that party of soldiers that left Chivington's Volunteers at Sand Creek!

The group was led by Colonel Reginald Saunders. A man from Alabama who fancied himself a Confederate hero. The entire group was from Alabama, Georgia, and Louisiana. They went to Fort Hays to await the next uprising of the Confederacy. The uprising never came!

Thanks to us and the wolves, the group perished one by one. All fourteen followers of Saunders would be turned to dust at our hands or the wolves. I took the last one, Colonel Saunders. The hero of the Confederacy and esteemed officer begged for his life before I drained his blood. It always amazed me that so many "strong" demons were actually cowards when death looked at them through Vampire or Wolf eyes. But it was at Fort Hays that we met one of the most

sinister of demons. Colonel George Armstrong Custer!

George A. Custer was a graduate of the White Man's West Point in 1861 at the start of their Civil War. He was breveted to Brigadier General of Volunteers at twenty-three and was involved in many famous campaigns of that war. He received the truce flag of the Confederates and was present at their surrender at Appomattox in 1865.

After the "War", Custer received an appointment as Lt. Colonel. He led the Seventh Calvary in the Indian campaigns during the 1860's and 1870's.

What made Custer so sinister was the fact he aspired to be "The Great Father", President. His use of reporters on his campaigns was done to document battles with the People. To assure his election in 1876 or 1880.

But Custer was a demon. He had married Elizabeth Custer, a female demon, with the hope of having hybrids. Elizabeth proved to be barren.

At Fort Hays when we first saw Custer, he was working on plans against the People. By 1868, Custer was planning a major campaign against the Cheyenne or Sioux by the end of the year.

Understand that when I talk of the People, I talk about not just the Cheyenne but all the tribal nations. If you look at the translations of the names of most of the tribes, you find they mean pretty much all the same. The People!

In October 1868, Custer got his wish for a campaign. Black Kettle and numerous other Cheyenne factions were converging on an area on the Washita River near what would later be known as Cheyenne, Oklahoma. In mid-November 1868, Custer and the Seventh Calvary left

Fort Hays headed towards that area in the Indian Territory.

Black Kettle was a leader of the Southern Cheyenne who professed peace. Because of his stance, many of the Warriors would not follow him. His Village consisted mainly of women and children with few Warriors. They were camping on the Washita for the winter. A few other Villages like my father's arrived in October 1868, to protect Black Kettle. Black Kettle was still a very well, respected Leader. Still the encampment's population had far more women and children and old people than Warriors.

Lone Wolf and I arrived in mid-November with our wolves. So did our children with their spouses and wolves. Our wolves told us that something big was going to happen and we were to protect and save as many of the People we could. We or any of the Warriors would not be able to stop what was going to happen.

Custer's scouts were following a Cheyenne Raiding Party that was terrorizing White Settlements along the Washita River. They came back to Custer and told him of a huge Cheyenne encampment on the Washita not more than three days' ride away. He led his troops in that direction. You see, Custer always reacted and rarely thought before attacking!

It was true, the Raiding Party had come to the encampment, but they left a couple of days later. They were long gone before Custer's arrival at Washita. On the morning of November 27, 1868, Custer and the Seventh Calvary surrounded the encampment and attacked it!

Custer had brought a handful of demons disguised as soldiers. Their mission was to steal maidens and take them to the Western Portal. There they would be impregnated by demons and the Evil One. It was our mission to stop them!

As always, the Whites said the Cheyenne fired the first shot. It was the Blue Coats! At Black Kettle's lodge, an American Flag was flying, and he came out when the first shots were fired. It was Sand Creek all over again. He pleaded with the troops to cease fire. Black Kettle was one of the first one's killed in the first volley. The Seventh Calvary had the new repeater rifles that fired rapidly into the Village. They were killing many women and children and old people. Far more than Warriors. The Warriors' single shot long rifles were no match for the repeaters.

We, the Spirit Warriors, concentrated on the escaping People and the Blue Coats. The wolves focused on the eight to ten demons trying to get young maidens under the age of twenty-five!

Six demons took off toward the West with maidens. He Wolf, She Wolf, Sacred Wolf, the Seventh Son, Dante, and Augustus went for the demons. All of us Spirit Warriors heard what the wolves were doing, and we headed toward them. Moving our horses alongside the wolves to help rescue the maidens.

She Wolf eased her way to the first demon's horse. She leaped on the horse's back and then, the demon's back. She ripped a huge chunk of the demon's neck, letting him bleed out. There was nothing the demon could do once ravaged by a Spirit Wolf but die! He was dead in a matter of seconds and turned to dust. She Wolf jumped off. Lone Wolf had eased his horse into the other galloping horse with the human maiden laid over it. He slowed the horse down so the maiden could mount it properly and led her to the fleeing People.

He Wolf and the other wolves did the same thing as She Wolf had done to her demon. All demons were killed by the wolves and had turned to dust. The remaining maidens were rescued, and they rode to the line of People that were fleeing the massacre! We saved many! But many died!

The soldiers were cleaning up the bodies as we watched from a knoll. They dug pits and threw the dead bodies into them. It was so sad! Then, the soldiers snaked their way southward, back towards Fort Hays. Lone Wolf was below the knoll making sure the last of the People had made their way to safety. I sat on my horse on that knoll watching the pits, the bodies, and the dirt that the soldiers were covering them up with.

"Well, Mystic Maiden Warrior? Do you think you can defeat the Evil One and his demons?"

It was Custer! He was on his horse. His silver-bladed saber drawn. His eyes were the blackest I had ever seen!

"Yes, we will! And we will destroy your Portals and your horrible Plan! We will stop you from getting maidens with child, Colonel Custer!"

Custer laughed! His smile was so evil!

"General Custer, Mystic! I am sure you and your half-wit children will destroy the Portals. But not before the Evil One returns to Earth to walk among those losers of humans. He will rule them and have so many new portals, Spirit Warriors will not be able to destroy them all. A new breed of demon is coming, Mystic. Ones that the Spirit Warriors will not be able to detect. They will walk among humans and kill all the People and their Spirit Warriors. Now it is time for

112

you to be the first killed! I will carry your head to the Evil One to show my loyalty!"

I readied myself for combat! Custer raised his saber to take my head. As the blade came down it met a lance. Lone Wolf's lance! He upended Custer off his horse. Custer scurried to his feet, trying to find his blade. Lone Wolf jumped off his horse with his silver bladed lance in his hand. He was to going to plunge that lance into Custer's heart. But a large number of soldiers came to Custer's aid. Lone Wolf jumped on his horse!

"Ride, Mystic, ride!"

And as we rode off towards the People! I heard Custer call out to me!

"Ride, Mystic! Hide, Mystic! I am coming for you! I will take your head! Mystic, Whore Bitch!"

We rode some distance from Custer and his men and stopped. Watching the soldiers depart, I was so angry and sad. I got down off my horse and sat on the ground. I started crying! Lone Wolf took me into his loving arms, trying to comfort me! There was no comforting me at that moment!

I cried for the People who lived! I cried for the People who died! But I cried most for Black Kettle! I cried for my father!

My Father defended the women and children. Especially my mother! My Mother watched in horror within fifty feet of her Lover. Several soldiers surrounded my father and shot into his body. I watched from afar as they shot him. I could not count the number of bullets that riddled his body. My Mother tried to run to him but was restrained by a number of women fleeing the horrific scene. They threw his dead body into one of the pits.

The thing about death and burial sites for the Cheyenne is once a person is buried or put on a scaffold, no one ever moves that person. So, my father was buried and there was nothing we could do about giving him a proper Cheyenne burial. The proper burial of a great Warrior with his weapons and other possessions to take into the afterlife. Disturb a dead person's body was like violating it.

We guided the survivors of Washita to various Villages from Colorado to the Black Hills. I took my mother to her People so she could heal. She never did! Love has a strange effect on people.

My children returned to their routines. Northern Warrior went to the Black Hills with Morning Star. Western Star and Douglass returned to San Francisco. Southern Warrior and Juanita went back to Dallas. And Eastern Star and Cody went back to the Mississippi River Boats. Every couple returned with their wolves.

As for Lone Wolf and I, we roamed the Plains. We killed demons as we found them. We searched the Silver Mines of Nevada, looking for the Western Portal. None was found!

Custer's words haunted me!

"The Evil One will return and find portals everywhere!"

What did that mean? She Who Speaks to the People had told me that once the Portals were destroyed, Lone Wolf and I would be mortal again! Did that mean, immortality would continue? I was fine with that as long as Lone Wolf was at my side. But if something happened to him?

"Maheo take me too"!

But today was a new day! The beginning of a new Journey! There were new adventures out there waiting for us. New journeys that need to be told! And I was going to tell them!

I walked out of our lodge with a new purpose! My face was painted for War! Half black and half white with red circles around my eyes! Spirit Warrior! Lone Wolf was painted the same. We had our weapons, our War Horses, our Wolves! Demons prepare to die! We

are coming for each of you! I am coming for you! I, Mystic Maiden

Warrior! Queen of the Spirit Warriors and Wolves! Half Vampire,

half Wolf. From this day forward, I would be known as The Spirit

Warrior-Wolf Queen!

Made in the USA
Middletown, DE
04 November 2022

14041932R00084